MEXICAN MASQUERADE (LA COMPARSA)

Latin American Literary Review Press

Yvette E. Miller

Editor

MEXICAN MASQUERADE (LA COMPARSA)

by
Sergio Galindo
Translated by Carolyn and John Brushwood

Latin American Literary Review Press
Series: Discoveries
Pittsburgh, Pennsylvania

The Latin American Literary Review Press publishes creative writing under the series title *Discoveries,* and critical works under the series title *Explorations.*

Copyright © 1984 by the Latin American Literary Review Press.

Library of Congress Cataloging in Publication Data
Galindo, Sergio.
    Mexican masquerade.

    (Discoveries)
    Translation of: La comparsa.
    I. Title. II. Series.
PQ7297.G23C613   1984   863   84-21826
ISBN 0-935480-17-X
Cover Design: Tina Matsch
This project is partially supported by grants from the National Endowment for the Arts in Washington, D.C., a Federal agency.
Mexican Masquerade can be ordered directly from the publisher:
    Latin American Literary Review Press
    P.O. Box 8385
    Pittsburgh, Pennsylvania 15218

To Alfredo Beltrán,
first reader of my work

> Loving people are like madmen —
> alone, alone, terribly alone —
> offering themselves, constantly giving,
> weeping because they leave love unsheltered.
>
> — Jaime Sabines, *Horal*

.

His return seemed inexplicably normal to Bartolomé. Of course, when one judges himself, he always tends to . . . Bartolomé heard his son, and said, «What?»

And the boy, struggling to carry a book on his shoulder, replied, «I'm going to put this away for you.»

Bartolomé ran, took the heavy book from him, put him back on the couch and threw himself on the hemp rug again where he had a magnificent observation point.

The wind rustled the flowers, the sun seemed to be wilting them as if they were suddenly dying in the prime of life — or do flowers commit suicide? — and the voice of the child taking in everything, demanding, «Pop, I'm going to put away your book. Look, Pop, I'll put it here so nobody else'll get it.» And he, Bartolomé, without seeing anything, knew he had to turn and say something.

«That's fine, dear.»

Absurd, absurd, trite and silly to say that.

Now slowly, very slowly the cat was coming toward them.

«Papá, Pop.»

«What?»

«Pop.»

A silence, the child tottered and started to climb the bookcase again looking for a new treasure. Bartolomé said to himself, «Either I'm drunk or nothing is going to happen to him.» And he looked at the garden and tried to think of his return that was so inexplicably normal.

He smoked. The morning — its light — was diminishing, making the area of shadow in his study larger and larger. It still isn't Spring. In a little while the bougainvillia will be completely covered with flowers and there won't be a single sad *tulipan*; the geraniums, the wisteria, the palms will be greener. Is Spring coming? Today's heat is false, a premonition. But I don't want to think about the weather.

I . . . my coming back . . . Jalapa . . . Jalapa again and as quiet as ever. Somewhere Barbara is fussing (I hear her, must be with the maid) and this is reality that seems strange to me now — inexplicably — because if it really were strange, I would have to begin at the beginning. And anyway there is no surprise and never has been. Everything is all planned. It is certain. A person defines his security and tranquility surely and tranquilly. I am only the product of my successful bunglings. I like that. It sounds intelligent. My successful bunglings . . . It's serious and has a certain moral force to say that my bunglings are . . . No, now it's a question of . . .

«You're drunk.»

Bartolomé raised his eyes and found her in her embroidered robe.

«You're beautiful.»

«And you are . . .»

«Intelligent. We both are, so you're not going to tell me what I don't want you to tell me and, besides, you wouldn't have any real reason . . .»

«Be quiet!»

«All right, now I'll give you the reason. You are the intelligent one . . . Pour me another rum.»

«Get it yourself.»

«What?»

«I'm giving you the chance to show you're intelligent, too.»

And Barbara, half joking and half serious, threw herself on the rug and curled up to avoid a possible push from Bartolomé. But he didn't move. Watching her, concentrating on where she was and what she was saying, he burst out laughing.

«You little devil, if I hadn't married you . . . Poor thing, if I weren't so,» he stood up and reached for the bottle of rum, «intelligent.»

«And so dear to me,» Barbara laughed, far removed from all that he was thinking, simply trying not to move in the terrible morning heat. «The worst in more than a year,» she had said that morning to Maria, the maid. «I'm not from around here, so I feel it more.» And then, immediately, she wanted to laugh at herself. At times she explained, «I can't laugh at Bartolomé.» And when she said it to herself (which was often), she laughed until she cried, to the astonishment (half pleasure-half fear) of Toni and the disapproval (which made her laugh more) of Ana.

She was wearing nothing but nylon panties and her silk robe. She felt in her body, breasts and below in her belly an innocent, odd tickling sensation.

«What's wrong?»

«Nothing.»

Bartolomé sighed. She wasn't laughing at him; he was sure of that. He said, «You're a liar. Nobody laughs at nothing.»

«It was the tickles.»

«What?»

«This.»

«Then get up . . . Or get dressed.»

«No, not today. Remember, it's a holiday . . . in this beautiful city of yours.»

«Don't criticize Jalapa,» he said and both started to laugh and embraced just as Ana looked up from her doll and said, pleadingly,

«Papá . . .»

And Toni, coming out of who-knows-what cave, cried,
«She's mine, Pop.»
Barbara and Bartolomé burst out laughing.
«My Electra and Oedipus. We are absolutely classical. Come on, kids.»
«Aren't you being a little professorial?» asked Barbara.
All four of them, hugging each other, laughed together.

* * *

«Señorita Alicia! Your father is calling from New York . . . Señorita!»
Alicia heard her call first when she was in the middle of the pool. She swam quickly. «Why?» she asked herself as she neared the edge. «An accident . . . something . . . maybe he needs money . . . it's just me . . . they want to know if I'm all right . . . no . . . could be Mamá . . . yes, an accident.» She started to run across the lawn.

In the opposite direction Señora Isunza ran also. The maid looked over the third floor balcony. She saw both of them running, one toward the other, like a movie, as if they were going to embrace. A movie in color, chrysanthemums, geraniums, acacias, all blooming prematurely. Señorita Alicia in her blue bathing suit. Señora Isunza in bishop's purple. In the background the pool of very clear green, its edge of red and white tiles.

«Hurry, hurry,» Señora Isunza cried. «He's on the phone.»

The maid saw Señora Isunza sway as she stopped suddenly, then put her hand to her breast while Alicia started down the path between the roses and was hidden from view.

Alicia pushed open the glass door. I'm going to get the carpet wet.

She said, «Yes . . . yes . . . hello . . . Alicia Esteva.»

The telephone operator, her voice sure, monotonous, efficient: «Señor Esteva is ready.»

«Papá?»

«Ali. Good morning. How are you?»

She sighed. She felt ridiculous.

«Fine. How are you?»

«Delighted with this trip. Today more than ever.»

«Oh?» Alicia asked and automatically, «Good. I'm glad. You startled me . . .»

«But don't you remember what day this is?»

«No . . . what?»

«Our anniversary. We've been married twenty-five years.»

«Oh, of course. What an idiot! I thought of it yesterday. How silly of me. Lots of love to both of you.»

«Thank you, my dear. Me, too. Your mother wants to talk to you. . . .Is there any news?»

«No, nothing. Everything's going fine. Oh, yesterday your architect friend, Señor Falcón, was killed in an accident.»

«Oh? I'm so sorry. How did it happen?»

«A car wreck at Sedeño Bridge.»

«Send a wreath. Your mother wants to talk to you. What do you want us to bring you?»

«Nothing. Whatever you like . . . Mamá . . . yes . . . yes . . . Fine . . . I'm getting your new carpet wet . . . I was in the pool . . . yes . . . yes . . . Congratulations.»

«Papá thought you might forget and so we called you. And I wanted to know how you were, and how are you?»

«Just fine. Carnival starts tomorrow and I'm planning to have a good time.»

«Now remember your dignity and behave yourself.»

«Yes, Mamá, yes. Remember this is long distance . . . . Congratulations to you both!»

«To the three of us, my dear, all three!»

«Yes, thank you.»

«Next summer you'll go with us.»

«Yes. Thank you.»

Alicia put the phone down firmly. She dried a tear and then the rest of her face.

«And how are they?» Señora Isunza asked, at her shoulder.

Without turning, Alicia said, «Fine. They called just to say you could have a day off, three days off. All of Carnival. I'll expect you Wednesday.»

«Me? Oh, how thoughtful of them! To call on account of me. Really?»

«Yes, you're free right now. Would you like me to lend you some money?»

«No . . . . well . . . yes . . . I, I mean I don't like to leave you alone.»

«Don't worry about me. I won't be alone. Carmela will come to stay with me. How much would you like?»

«I . . . ,» Señora Isunza was bewildered. «Well, a hundred — fifty pesos.»

«I'll give you a hundred. If you need more, tell me. I'm going to get dressed.»

* * *

Arnaldo Wells woke with an awesome hangover. He thought twice and before the third time, when he would undoubtedly decide to go back to sleep, jumped out of bed, stepped on the cold, dirty tiles and ran to the bathroom.

He tested the water. It was hot. He got into the shower and, scrubbing himself front and back, made one of his most common observations, «Sin is cleansed with soap and water.»

* * *

«It's wonderful, astonishing, how beautiful you are!»

«I don't see why you should be so astonished,» Zenaida said, still looking in the mirror. She leaned her head to one side. Her wide, green eyes reminded her satisfyingly of Vivian Leigh in *Lady Hamilton*, the scene where she writes the letter. She arched her eyebrows and said to herself, «I'm lovely.»

«What?» Doña Pilar asked.

«All my life you've told me that I am beautiful, precious, marvelous. Now you don't have any reason to be surprised that I really am.»

Doña Pilar laughed. «What modesty! My dear daughter, you are . . . like me.»

«No, I'm not like you,» Zenaida answered, trying some other earrings. «But I'm not blind. I know I'm pretty. There's nothing surprising about it.»

With her mouth still open, Doña Pilar laughed and kept on looking at her daughter. She felt speechless but had to say something. «If Eugenio sees you, he'll tell you you're exactly like his mother.»

«Then he'll be lying, too . . . Papá is much darker than we are and I don't believe his mother was as light as he says.»

Doña Pilar was disconcerted. Every time she tried to share — «the way it ought to be» — her daughter's world, she felt harshly excluded, deprived absolutely of any opportunity to penetrate farther than Zenaida would permit. She picked up a black dress and put it on. Doña Pilar smiled. There was something magic in everything Zenaida did. Any old rag could transform her into still another mystery, still another delight. Zenaida is the mystery of a thousand paths. A labyrinth. Now she had transformed herself again and was going through her jewelry case. A long pearl necklace appeared in her hands and she skillfully started twining it in her hair. . . . Doña Pilar's mouth opened wider. She only managed to murmur, «Oh . . .» It was as if she saw herself young again and a thousand times lovelier than when she was young.

«Can I help you?»

«No, I can do it myself.»

Doña Pilar picked up the net with sequins and caressed it. «I hope it's warm tomorrow,» she said. «If it's not, you could catch cold with only this on.» She murmured slowly, as if she were writing it, «the mystery of a thousand paths.»

* * *

«Maria is perfect,» Barbara said, leaning back on his shoulder. «Right out of the movies. She knows when to take them to get candy. . . . Don't you think?»

Bartolomé agreed with an affectionate grunt, rubbed against her and thought how right she was.

«It's because she belongs to the Catholic Morality League of Jalapa . . . and that's why she quickly removed our innocent children from the spectacle.»

«You devil!»

She bit her finger, pressed against his silk shirt, asked with feigned innocence, «You're not embarrassed?»

«Bitch. No. I respect myself. And I respect Maria's principles.»

«Don't drink any more.»

«Don't be so conventional. There are no witnesses. We're just the two of us alone after . . .»

«Don't be crude.»

«Don't be conventional . . . 'My mama done told me. When I was in . . .'»

«You see?»

«Oh, it's Carnival and it's hot and I've got ideas.»

«You've got two children.»

«Barbara, *please*. Listen to me. You know that . . .»

«That you're drunk, Bar.»

«My name is Bar . . . a bar is supposed to be full of liquor, isn't it?»

«Please. It's very early.»

Suddenly Bartolomé realized everything was cozy and permissive, even his wife.

«You know something . . .» he started to say, and a smile came to his lips. «Jalapa and London have certain similarities because . . .»

Barbara rose suddenly. She knew the theme.

«You're drunk.»

He, from his position on the jute rug, watched her walk surely and rapidly inside.

«I was drunk ten minutes ago and it didn't matter then!»

Maria and the children came back with their candy. Bartolomé got up quickly, buttoned his pants and ran into the garage. They came in shouting, «Papá! . . Mamá!»

Bartolomé turned the switch and the motor started. Maria closed the doors and with practiced smoothness said, «Come, children, let's go up to find your mother.»

* * *

After breakfast Alicia sat down to go over the weekly bills, sign checks, order a wreath — «The largest you have, please.» She called Señor Olmos to say, «Papá just called me; he is fine. He sent you his best regards. I told him everything was going just fine.» A few minutes later Clementina Pereda called, asked how she was and said, «Is there anything I can do for you?» «Nothing, thank you. Mamá called me about an hour ago from New York, she sends you love and asked about your typhoid.» «Better now, thank heaven.» Then Carmela. «All three days? Mamá will be furious, but I'll come.» Next, Daniel: «Right at five. Everyone is coming.» «O.K.»

Señora Isunza had changed to a suit. Alicia gave her a hundred pesos. «Before you go, please ask the chauffeur to buy me two *capuchones.*»

«Two what?»

«*Capuchones.* Hoods. Disguises — the ones that cover you completely. It's Carnival. Remember?»

The idea excited her. To be hidden, covered completely . . . Alicia Esteva turned into a stranger, her identity hidden by the hood . . . covered from head to foot . . . Alicia Esteva . . . Alicia Nobody . . . Alicia Everybody . . . Nobody . . . Everybody . . . All Jalapa wondering who I am . . . wonderful Jalapa . . . hidden Jalapa . . . hidden Alicia. But why do I . . . I shouldn't be cruel with her . . . Every time I say something, she looks terrified. And the poor woman is so . . . All because I was so dumb. For me to think they were calling for something important. But no, they had to remind me that I forgot. And then the way he took it about the architect, to say «Oh? I'm so sorry.» If I had said it had rained a lot, he would have said the same, «Oh? I'm so sorry.» And after all, what does it matter to me? Less than to him! If I had said he was killed with four women and maybe one of them was a friend of Papá's . . . Yes, that's what I should have done. That would have stopped him. «You know what, dear Papá? He was killed with one of your girl friends.»

Alicia started to laugh and the chauffeur laughed, too, and then said, «Do you want to give me the money to buy the masks?»

* * *

Adriana said, «The children send love and kisses. Mamá will bring them in two weeks.»

She put her arm around Tino's waist and they started to walk behind the porter as he ran toward a cab.

«Has the furniture come?»

«Early this morning,» Tino replied. «Everything is in the living room and the hall. You've got enough work for ten days.»

«I'm still tired from packing and now I have to start all over again.»

Tino opened the door of the cab. Briefly Adriana had her first view of the city: a wide avenue, modern houses. She looked up: the sun, a blue sky. A week before she had complained to Leandro about the air in Mexico City and he answered, «You'll love Jalapa.» The air was perfumed. Tino kissed her. Adriana embraced him and didn't cry because Tino didn't like it. She closed her eyes and said to herself, «For a long time . . . a long time.»

«Tonight we'll have dinner at Leandro's. Sara, his wife, is having a party in your honor. Big celebration tomorrow. Carnival starts here.»

«But it's Lent.»

«Yes. Do you like it?» Tino was referring to Jalapa. He nodded vaguely toward the streets.

«Yes,» she said, but she was referring to him.

*　*　*

The bar was dimly lighted. A drunk kept up his complaint, «She doesn't realize that's exactly what keeps us apart.»

«Right,» said Bartolomé. «You're absolutely right.»

He started drumming his fingers rhythmically on the table. «To have come out for this,» he said to himself, and then while he repeated the melody, «Jalapa is a prison,» went to the phone again. He crossed the dingy hall of the Casino, entered the shadow of the small salon and very slowly, to avoid mistakes, dialed Arnaldo Wells' number. The phone buzzed repeatedly in his right ear. I have the advantage, he told himself as he returned, that no one knows I'm drunk. It's too early for this lousy city. Its good and honorable drunks start after twelve. Except, of course, this guy.

The guy looked at him at length, so long that it seemed he was not going to say anything else and Bartolomé was at the point of being grateful for his silence when the other continued, «And if I tell you she doesn't understand me, it's because . . .»

Bartolomé dropped his glass and the waiter ran to his side. The trick was still effective.

«You didn't get cut?»

«No, no. It was clumsy of me . . .»

Carefully the waiter started to gather up the pieces of glass. Bartolomé, embarrassed, said, «I must go.»

Outside the sun was shining brilliantly. Jalapa could be beautiful. A clear, very blue sky enveloped her, almost artificially, almost as if she were a toy. He stood there on the main corner, swaying. In front of him the National Bank of Mexico suffered an oscillating earthquake. If I were a poet, he told himself, I would manage to have an earthquake right now. Immediately the idea bored him. He yawned and everything seemed to him — himself first of all — an idiotic fraud. Now he was going to talk with someone. With no one. With anyone: «You know, the thing is I don't accept triumphs as triumphs. Do you understand me, really?»

Clementina Pereda stopped in front of him.

«And your wife?»

«Triumphant, absolutely triumphant.»

«Yes?»

«Yes, really happy. She likes this season. She likes Jalapa.»

«Oh?»

«More than I.»

«Really?» Clementina asked, as happy as if someone had annoyed her. And, shaking her orange cloth hat, repeated, «Really?».

There she was in front of him, the famous, official spinster of Jalapa, disposed to feel she herself was Jalapa and flattered or insulted by any nonsense said for or against her home town.

«Really. She loves Jalapa as much as I do.»

«Oh, how charming! She's so lovely. I want to invite her to Guild meeting. Won't you tell her?»

«Of course.» He saw a group of students coming close and turned to Clementina, smiling sweetly, «I have to go. I was waiting for them.»

Clementina stayed a few more minutes watching as he went up to the group of young people. She smiled. Jalapa is growing every day! She went in to the store to make her purchases.

* * *

Luis Rentería carefully closed *The System of Procedural Law* by Canelutti and left it on the sofa. He rubbed his eyes, not remembering a single line he had read. He stood up. His limp brown hair fell over his forehead, a pale and shining forehead, which he observed in the tin-framed mirror. He saw his short, thin brows, grey eyes, his long, straight nose, very thin cheekbones, and pale lips.

The wind stirred the venetian blinds and on the mirror waves of light and shade distorted his image. The apartment was so small a slight breeze seemed like a hurricane. He started his search above the bookcases and on the table and chairs, turning them around, brushing off piles of books and notebooks, cups, glasses. Why do I always lose my comb? He went in to the bedroom and then continued the fruitless search in the bathroom. Not there either. He ran his fingers through the hair that fell stubbornly over his brow. He went back in the bedroom, opened the top drawer of the dresser and looked over the contents: socks, letters, handkerchiefs, playbills, old menus, newspaper clippings, cuff links, champagne corks. Something had a metallic sound. He investigated: the medal . . . He took it in his hands and read, as if he had never seen it before, «First Place. Oratory Contest. Institutional Revolutionary Party.» And in almost invisible letters «Luis Rentería Nieto, Student in the School of Law.» He threw it to the back of the drawer, and went to the kitchen, even though he didn't expect to find his comb there. But it was. He moved a box of detergent and picked it up.

He turned on the sink faucet and stuck his head under; then, dripping, went to the bathroom, threw a towel around his shoulders, took a handful of perfumed liquid and rubbed it on his hair.

The phone rang while he was changing his shirt.

«Luis? . . This is Jacobo.»

«O.K. I'm ready.»

«In half an hour at El Emir.»

«Ciao.»

«Ciao.»

Luis turned to look at himself in the mirror. He stretched out on the couch. His hand fell near a piece of white paper. He picked it up. The same name over and over in different kinds of letters: Margarita, Margarita, Margarita. He balled up the paper and threw it on the floor.

* * *

«I, Mayor of this city by action of the PRI and of his Excellency, the Governor . . .»

Genaro Almanza pretended to make a joke, but really the satisfaction of the event made him perspire happily. His hands grasped the iron balcony. He felt sweat moisten the surface and he loosened his fingers. Some clouds hid the sun and the park below was shady and fresh. The tops of araucaria trees reached farther than Genaro and Leandro could see. At almost their level the jacarandas were forgetting winter. The rest of the park was lost in walls of carnival stands: masks, confetti, beer, plastic toys, a shooting gallery (the prizes: bottles of Havana rum and of Rompope, clay dolls — a fat man defecating and a China Poblana doll with the features of Maria Félix), beer, Hawaiian leis, masks, false noses, spectacles, crepe paper hats, beer, a shooting gallery, beer, tacos and barbecue, beer, dried fruits, plums, dates, «Corinthian» raisins (all covered with flies), gilded and silvered confetti, necklaces, bracelets, rings, mirrors, beer, mechanical toys, cotton candy, beer, brassieres and stockings, confetti, hot snacks, beer, beer, beer, beer . . . Farther along against the background of the lower level: a merry-go-round, a tilt-a-whirl, two ferris wheels, a pendulum, a rock 'n roll, an octopus, a crack-the-whip, turtles, ducks, planes, cars for the children, a funny house, a headless woman, snake show, Mara the fortune teller. Everything. In the middle of the park food stands (tended by queers «from Guadalajara») decorated with paper banners and ads for Superior beer.

«Look,» Genaro said, «our beautiful Juárez Park turned into a dump.»

«It's our beautiful Carnival.»

«This year there will be lots of floats.»

«Yes, like always, from Veracruz.»

«And from here, too. The city is going to have an enormous canoe of flowers from the whole region, from here, Coatepec, Córdoba, Fortín, San Andrés, from the whole state, even vanilla blooms from Papantla. A giant cone will be covered with flowers and a mermaid will be on top,»

Leandro laughed.

«And what is a mermaid doing in a canoe?»

«The mermaid is Zenaida López.»

«Ah ha! That explains everything. I don't suppose they're going to cover her legs.»

«No, she's going to wear tights with spangles.»

«Zenaida López has her career all set.»

«She's had it set for quite a while,» Genaro said and smiled as if he were his own accomplice.

«Let's hope it doesn't rain.»

«I don't think it will this year. Look, the sun's out again and even stronger.»

The park sparkled anew. Balloon clusters and hoods of automobiles gleamed in the streets. A marimba started to play and Jalapa seemed, suddenly, happy and simple.

«Don't you like this?» asked Mayor Genaro Almanza drumming on the balcony.

«I don't like *that*,» Leandro said.

Below in the park a man dressed in black moved forward with difficulty.

* * *

«Women shouldn't even have names before they're thirty-five. Right?»

Jacobo Páez looked at him. He smiled and said, «Right, maestro.»

Bartolomé realized he was definitively drunk and that it was all Barbara's fault. No wife should permit her husband to go out with more than seven drinks on an empty stomach. But then there was no reason to blame Barbara. She didn't even know he'd had seven.

«The important thing is the effect,» he told the cab driver some minutes later as they were passing in front of the park.

Bartolomé remembered that he had a car and that he was a respected professor. He ordered, «To the Casino.»

At the corner he saw Jacobo and his friends with some other students.

* * *

The man in black, young, very tall and thin, rebuffed a child with sticky hands who wanted to grab him. He tried to smile. But it was too hot, the starch in his collar tortured his throat. Two streams of sweat ran between his shoulder blades down to his belt. His nylon trousers (a present from his mother) bothered him — itching heat misery, too tight, too conscious of his wretched body. At the beer stands men laughed loudly. Children screamed, pursued by mothers, maids. One group of youngsters (ten, twenty) stood in his way. The man in the black suit cut over to a side street and immediately found himself trapped by something worse. A group of masked dancers followed by fifty, maybe a hundred, kids. He jumped over a flower border to get out of the way. He thought they would keep on the way they were going, but no. They stationed themselves right there so he had no escape. At his back the thorns of a rose bush cut off his flight. He stepped back, a small step so as not to fall or step on those shouting in front of him.

A pair of mulattoes were dancing, a clean, shiny sweat bathing their bodies. Twisting rivers, the music a provocative roar. The woman, the man, the woman the man spurred on by laughs and shouts.

He lifted his face. I'm not going to look back any more. He saw the walls of the Municipal Palace, and on the main balcony the body, the laugh of Leandro Montes. Below the woman continued her attack and the man, shouting, seemed beaten and stretched his arms to the public (to him) once and then again, each time more frenzied. And the maracas and a cowbell clanging, mercilessly, and the rhythm grimaces of the spectators. The man in the black suit felt the thorns dig into him. He stepped on the bush and escaped.

* * *

Bartolomé stopped the car. He closed the windows, checked to see that all the doors were locked and picked up his newspaper. As he went up the steps, it occurred to him there could be no better way to show he was sober than to whistle loudly and proceed with paper in hand as if he were reading it.

And actually he did read: «Terrible tragedy. Falcón, local architect, suffers horrible death in company of four women.» «Last night after an ill-fated orgy, the well-known architect, Julio Falcón, perished in an auto accident.» He skipped some lines and read, «He was accompanied by four women of doubtful reputation, fading flowers who came to their end . . .»

Bartolomé laughed, felt completely sober and handed the paper to Barbara. She took it unenthusiastically but could not reproach him for anything. Bartolomé walked perfectly, picked Toni up and dropped into an armchair, where Ana jumped into his lap.

«Tomorrow I'll take you to Carnival and you'll see. . . there'll be witches

20

and goblins and . . .»

Later on, Barbara, wisely and silently reconciled with him, sat beside him. They were quiet for a while, not looking at each other. Both looking at the garden. Bartolomé said, «I knew that architect. . . He's a friend of my family.»

«You'll have to send a wreath.»

«And that is that.»

«Sara called. She wants us to come to dinner tonight.»

«To start celebrating Carnival?»

«To meet Tino's wife. She must have come today.»

* * *

«Carnival starts tomorrow. It's very strange — Carnival during lent. They've explained it to me. If they had Carnival at the same time in Veracruz and Jalapa, the one here would be a disaster and the one in Veracruz would make less money. Several years ago they held the one in Jalapa a week before (the one in Veracruz was at the regular time) but the mayor of Veracruz protested because their intake was cut, so the result is they have three days of orgy after Ash Wednesday.

I hope you're not too astonished. I just want to have a good time and think this is my chance. In the month and a half I've been here I've made friends with a very agreeable group — mostly University people. Maybe one will become your son-in-law.

Come for Holy Week.

Lots of love and kisses,
Margarita

* * *

Clementina Pereda raised the napkin to her mouth and while pretending to wipe it, adjusted her dentures. Her gums were so tender the pipian seeds hurt them.

Doña Hermila offered her more.

«No,» Clementina said with a charming smile, «everything is so delicious, but I couldn't eat another bite.»

An implacable silence fell over the dining room. Little by little everyone heard clearly the buzzing of the flies and the ill-bred chewing of Don Pedro. Clementina felt obliged to say something.

«I saw Bartolomé Soto downtown today, as young and handsome as always. Do you know Barbara?»

«Yes,» Doña Hermila said, «I met her at your house.»

«They say Bartolomé is a Communist,» Don Pedro exclaimed and belched.

Efrén grimaced and the mouthful of food came up in his throat. He took a sip of wine and swallowed again. Papá is a pig, he said to himself and added. It's Lent, it's Lent, but that doesn't matter. He's always coarse and vulgar.

«What is a Communist, Papá?»

Don Pedro flushed and disgustedly swallowed a piece of gristle before saying brusquely, «Well, what a thing to ask me. I, the least educated one here, am not going to explain what a Communist is to someone who has studied as much as you have.»

«Pedro,» Doña Hermilla begged, «remember that you are speaking to Efrén.»

Again Clementina felt the need to break the tension.

«A Communist, I suppose, is someone who belongs to the Communist party.»

«Exactly, Clementina,» Efrén said, «that's a good answer.»

«Of course, of course. That goes without saying.»

«Who would like some stewed peaches?» Doña Hermila asked.

«Give me some more of that,» Don Pedro said and peacefully probed his decayed teeth with tongue and fingers.

Efrén bit his napkin. He remembered when, many years ago, he had complained about one of his father's customs. It was at the house on Hidalgo Street in the inside garden. Don Pedro had unfastened his fly and started to urinate against the fence. Efrén, then twelve years old, had blushed, «Papá, you don't do that . . .» And Don Pedro calmly, «Bah. In Spain, in my village, everyone does it and no one even notices.» Efrén answered immediately, «Here the burros and dogs do it in the streets, too.» Even though she ran, Doña Hermila couldn't save him from the first blow and Efrén spit blood.

Clementina Pereda had a sharp sense that told her when something untoward was happening, something that could upset things and produce a violent scene and for the third time, she opened her mouth.

«Aren't you burning up in that black suit, Efrén?» and immediately corrected herself, «Pardon me, I mean Father Efrén.»

«Clementina, for heaven's sake,» he begged. «Don't call me Father. And I'm not burning up.»

«It's so hot,» Doña Hermila said, and somehow let the bowl of peaches fall to the floor.

Don Pedro exploded, «Idiot, clumsy fool!»

Clementina could not admit defeat. She wiped off some spots of syrup and tried again, «Did you know about those women and Señor Falcón?»

Hermila could endure no more and cried, «Clementina, please. This is my birthday and it's Lent. Let's think about something more pleasant and suitable.»

«Well,» Don Pedro said, «it seems to me very suitable that those four women died all at once. How many old women have to keep on forever with a sickness that never kills them? Tell me, Efrén, which is more merciful?»

The maid came in with the demitasse cups.

«Bring the cognac,» Don Pedro ordered.

Tirelessly Clementina tried to make conversation. She told herself, Everyone is going to think Don Pedro is a drunkard. (She herself was the first one to think so, but one shouldn't judge a neighbor). Really there are many worse. Ah, that will do it! Innocently Clementina exclaimed, «By the way, you know what they say? That Barbara, Bartolomé's wife and Leandro's wife, Sara, also drink too much.»

She smiled at her success. No one had noticed how cleverly she changed the subject.

Clementina's «also» made Hermila and her son blush (for different reasons), but Don Pedro, outside the conflict, agreed, «You can't believe anything. They say the same thing about me.»

* * *

«Be serious, please,» Jacobo ordered. «Stop acting like children. To their health and may they be eternal.»

«May they live in the minds and hearts of the men of Mexico!» Hernán shouted and burst out laughing.

«And of the women!»

«Right — a worthy example for Mexican womanhood,» Luis exclaimed.

Jacobo ordered more rum. He enjoyed amusing himself and amusing others. Antonio, the bartender, laughed and made comments to the two customers at the bar. Facing toward the busy street Jacobo watched the cars and buses moving constantly. At times some child stuck his head in the door, his face covered by a mask of a skull or a witch, shrieked stridently and happily fled. Jacobo made faces at them. Thumbs at his temples, hands moving like butterflies, he twisted his eyes and mouth and anticipated the cry of the child with a louder one of his own. The children made insulting gestures and ran away delighted. Antonio brought three more rums.

«They died on the field of battle.»

«Almost died for their country.»

«To their health.»

«This is an extrarodinary day,» Hernán said. «In time historians will call it 'an unforgettable Saturday'.»

«'A singular beginning to Carnival',» Luis went on, as though he were reading. «'In the year of our Lord, 1959, in the beautiful city of Jalapa'.»

«You and I could write a testimonial,» Jacobo said to Hernán, «and give it in a History seminar at mid-term. But we need to do research. It would be very good.»

«The best.»

«Very good. Very, very good and they would give us fellowships to Europe immediately as outstanding, brilliant students.»

«We'll get doctorates in some Parisian bordello and return as full time professors in the College of Philosophy and Letters.»

«There aren't any bordellos in Paris.»

«A cultural deficiency! They'll never be able to have an 'unforgettable Saturday' there.»

«Never.»

«We decree that this day shall be named 'Whores' Day' and we will erect a monument with four high crosses.»

«Immense, immense, and on the tips we will put beacons — four beacons that can be seen from Veracruz. So the tourists that arrive by ship will ask, 'What is that?'. The Captain will clear his throat before replying, 'The Monument to. . . «Whores' Day». . . . It's about 75 miles from here, in Jalapa. . . . Jalapa is the cultural capital of the state' and he will spit with satisfaction.»

«On the crosses we can have portraits of them, in bas relief.»

«But something special. For instance, while working.»

«That's it! Each one in her most successful position.»

«It could be a tourist attraction of the first order. It could be the beginning of a period of prosperity and riches for the city. Later other monuments could be built just like them and perhaps one day Jalapa will be more famous than Pompeii.»

«Jalapa, the vicious.»

«Jalapa, the rotten.»

«Jalapa, the prostitute.»

«Then, as the years go by, when people hear about the City of Flowers, they will think it means the girls.»

The three laughed with the two customers and the bartender.

«Another round, on me,» one of the customers ordered. He nudged his companion. «I remember when we were students.»

«So all four of them died?» his friend asked.

«All four women and Falcón, the owner of the car.»

«What I wonder,» said the bartender serving the rum, «is what kind of a guy would want four of them at the same time. But they say he was always that way. He played around with them all, and took good care of them, too.»

«I don't believe it,» said the man in the straw hat. «It's too much for one stud. I knew a guy once who could take on two at a time and satisfy them both, but four!»

«No, man. Who?»

«They told me that once this type I'm telling you about . . .»

The children, now a group of six or seven, appeared in the doorway and shouted insults at Jacobo. He got up and ran toward them. They ran away shrieking with laughter. Jacobo stopped at the entrance. He had no intention of leaving the shade. The heat and exertion made him sweat, and he wiped his forehead with a damp handerchief. A Ford convertible full of students stopped when they saw him.

«Jacobo! Come go to Sedeño, to the bridge! Come on!»

«They say there's still blood.»

«And muddy brains.»

«Want to go?»

«No,» he yelled, waving his handkerchief and they left.

He laughed. Some were wearing paper hats and masks. They were singing «Rosita Alvirez.» He pretended to chase the children once more and they again scattered with a great clamor.

«Play a record,» Luis shouted.

Jacobo dropped a coin in the juke box. «The Martians are coming . . .» Suddenly he started dancing, completely caught up by the music, his whole body swaying in the rhythm. Hernán joined him. Luis, older than they, watched them. I'm going to get drunk, he thought, and laughed. He began singing and drumming on the table — «Ricachá, Ricachá, Richachá. That's what they call it in Martian.»

«Hey, you guys!» called the bartender. «This gentleman here is inviting you to have a drink.»

«Felipe Gómez at your service. And my friend is Isidro Nervo.»

Luis stood up also and they shook hands.

«What are you studying?»

«I'm in Law,» Luis said. «The others are in History.»

«We went to high school here years ago and now we work on a ranch in Paso del Toro.»

«We come twice a year, for Carnival and at Christmas.»

«You can really have a great time here!»

«Of course,» the bartender interjected, «we have four whores and a wife for every man.»

A woman came out from the back room — a good looking woman, about thirty years old.

«Not that you could take care of that many,» she exclaimed, then turned and disappeared.

«She's equal to six,» the bartender explained with a wink and they all burst out laughing.

«You can see that,» said Hernán between laughs.

Antonio, the bartender, flushed angrily.

«He was referring to her character,» Jacobo said and scarcely finished the explanation when the three looked at each other and started laughing.

Isidro Nervo and Felipe Gómez did not understand but smiled and then smiled more broadly and finally laughed when they saw the bartender laughing also.

«You know, boys,» Antonio said, serving himself another half glass of rum, «if ever you don't have enough money and want a few drinks, come to see me. . . .»

His wife didn't come out again, but her voice carried from the next room.

«Don't drink any more, Antonio.»

«It's my first one,» he yelled back.

Hernán went to the juke box and played another record. Antonio, without being asked, began to serve another round.

«This one's on me,» Isidro Nervo said, and threw down a hundred peso bill.

«We've found a sucker,» Jacobo said quietly to Luis.

A furious rock and roll number made it impossible for Antonio's wife to hear anything and she didn't know that after Isidro Nervo's round, her husband served double shots. Felipe Gómez remembered when he was a student and one day they had a terrific strike, then he ordered some more drinks.

Jacobo blinked. It was almost five o'clock in the afternoon and he didn't want to get drunk. He had promised to meet the others at Alicia's house and anyway, the people in the bar had turned out not to be very interesting. With relief he saw the convertible stop again at the entrance to the bar. His friends got out noisily, blinded for a moment when they first came in to the shade.

«Everyone from Jalapa is there.»

«It's a great party. Really good. Probably the best party during Carnival.»

«Who's treating?»

«Is there any whiskey?»

«Give him some tequila.»

«Today we're drinking to the men left behind.»

«In this Carnival we ought to wear black ties.»

The owner of the car, a redhead named Batuta, ordered cognac for everybody.

«Jacobo, come here, with us.»

«I have a spot for you between my legs.»

«Bravo for Batuta! A real genius!»

«Tell another joke Batuta. Or I won't sit on your lap.»

Batuta flushed happily. He liked being popular.

«Another bottle for my friends.»

«Bring it, Antonio. He's not joking. His father's a millionaire.»

«The people pay.»

«Yes, let Batuta pay.»

* * *

«Yes, Mother,» Daniel said.

Lucia sat up in bed. She rested her elbow on the green satin pillow. Her eyes grew large.

«But, my dear,» she cried. «It's not a question of admitting I'm right just because I'm your mother. You must understand I am not thinking of myself, but you . . .»

Daniel went out. Lucia stretched out in the bed and closed her eyelids tightly. I am not sorry for anything, she told herself. It's all . . . it's all . . . it's all human stupidity.

The afternoon light entered insistently through the heavy curtains — the rays, tirelessly stabbing, at times reached her eyes. She thought about getting up. But no. She was very tired. And out loud she said, «I am not tired, but I don't want to move.»

* * *

«Today,» Alicia said, as she finished combing her hair. «Just so I wouldn't forget they've been married twenty-five years. Their silver anniversary. How corny! I'll bet you tonight they'll go to a night club and they'll show my picture and they'll say, 'She's our only daughter. She lives in Mexico, in Jalapa.'»

Carmela laughed and said, «Sometimes you're so American.»

Alicia flushed. «Why? Why do you say that?»

«Because you talk and act like a child in an American movie, like the story of the poor little rich girl deserted by her miserable millionaire parents traveling around the world. As obvious as that.»

«Idiot!»

«And you, nutty, sentimental, trite — it bothers you that your mommy and daddy have left you alone because you think for this sacred twenty-fifth anniversary you ought to give them an elegant party and all the families in Jalapa would bring silver gifts.»

«How horrible!»

«How charming, you mean! A fine marriage, a lovely daughter. The only thing lacking is the little grandmother and the whole scene is completely Mexican. I mean, for Americans. In the movies.»

Carmela started laughing and Alicia forgave her everything.

Now they were both ready. They left Alicia's room and went into the hall and down the huge, circular marble staircase.

Carmela said, «See, everything makes you the girl in the picture. Just look at the scene — pure Hollywood . . . here you could film 'Gone With The Wind,' or 'Camille', since nothing is authentic. That's what would occur to the first intelligent movie director who came here. I swear right here, just as it is, you could film 'Maria Candelaria' or anything else you liked.»

«Carmela,» Alicia begged, in her most proper voice. And then, as they walked across the grass toward the swimming pool, «You're acting, too. You're pretending you're one of the four women who died today and you're coming here to tell me what you think of me and shock me.»

«Those miserable women again!» Carmela shouted, throwing herself on the grass.

«Those poor things! One of them was probably my father's mistress.»

«Even worse!» Carmela said, rolling over.

«You devil!» Alicia shouted and jumped on top of her.

They rolled over and over until they reached the edge of the pool.

«If anyone sees us,» Carmela said, straightening her skirt, «they'll think we're a couple of Lesbians.»

Alicia laughed.

«A beautiful pair of young Lesbians . . .» Then, suddenly serious, «The most accurate part is the Lesbians, because we're not young any more.»

«Look,» Carmela said, brushing off her dress, «don't get tragic. Think of Clementina Pereda and your problem is solved. Anyway, two twenty-one year old girls . . .»

«Twenty-three,» Alicia corrected her.

«Two twenty-one year old girls,» Carmela repeated, «and virgins by choice, have nothing to worry about in this beautiful city of flowers.»

Alicia had sat down. She was looking at the water in the pool. She said, «I swear I wish I could be one of those women . . . and Daniel would go to bed with me.»

«And they would make him marry you.»

«No. I mean Daniel and lots of others, Bartolomé and . . . lots.»

Carmela stood up. The sun was in her eyes. «That's a lie,» she said. «A pious lie of modern spinsters. Neither of us was born to be a prostitute.»

«Don't be vulgar.»

«You mean, don't be low class. But really, at times, I'm very low class.»

Both of them, very slowly, started to walk toward the front garden. The wind had stopped. Heat pressed down heavily. Even the water of the fountain lacked freshness. Sweating, they sat down in some metal chairs under a willow. The music of a Charleston came toward them.

Alicia pressed her foot down beside her chair to make a bell ring in the kitchen.

«My house is so modern, so newly rich.»

«Have you noticed,» Carmela asked, «that what we call modern started before we were born — in the Twenties?»

«Yes.»

«All is lost! There's nothing new!»

«Yes, atomic bombs.»

«Big deal. I mean, for you and for me.»

The cook came toward them.

«Please bring us two gins with lemon juice.»

«And lots and lots of ice,» Carmela said.

Before and after the drinks there was a long silence. Both were looking at the garden, the nearest branches of the swaying willow, then the lawn, broken in its monotony by the rose bushes and then, above a line of purple hills, the sky.

Suddenly the strident noise of a car stopping, screeching to a halt.

«Only Batuta would do that,» Alicia said.

A few seconds passed. Then the doorbell rang. They saw the cook going to answer. Neither said anything until they heard Hernán's voice.

«It's them.»

«Yes.»

And they started walking toward the entrance.

*　*　*

Don Pedro Ferrón really didn't understand a Retreat — thinking of one's sins, repenting, taking Communion regularly, going into seclusion — all those things that his wife, Doña Hermila, called «spiritual.»

«It's all gibberish to me,» he said, serving himself another brandy. He saw his son go out accompanied by Clemen and Doña Hermila. «The three of them together. Same as always,» he said and took another sip. «The same ten years ago, or twenty . . . He always went to church with them. A vocation? Laziness! It he were a real man, he wouldn't wear long skirts. Those priests and sissies — God save us from both!» And Don Pedro finished his drink and poured another.

The dog heard the sound of the front door closing and ran barking. No one was there. She started running again, stopped in the middle of the corridor, sniffed around and went up to the terrace where Don Pedro was.

«Who was it, little girl?» he asked, patting her. «No one? Have they left us alone? Yes, sweetie . . . but . . . but . . .»

He thew himself down on the glider. The weight of his two hundred pounds and suddenness of his fall made it swing dangerously. Don Pedro lost his balance momentarily, thought he was going to fall, tried awkwardly to avoid it and the glider slid across the marble terrace until it hit the planter of chrysanthemums. He burst into a sweat. The planter made a weak barrier, a decoration only, something that — once the money had been spent by Doña Hermila, who insisted on having this new collection of plants — had kept him from building a strong, expensive fence. His forehead, neck and armpits were bathed in sweat. He took out his handkerchief and wiped his face. It bothered him to be a coward. And, even worse, it bothered him that Efrén had inherited his cowardice. His cowardice wasn't his own — «the poor child, always so delicate!» — but Pedro Ferrón's. That was the reason he was quiet every time Efrén came home with blood on his clothes, every time he saw his eyes wide with fright, every time he heard him — that sharp, shrill, feminine cry. That cry that was his own, belonged to *him*, to Pedro, not to poor little Efrén, as he used to call him privately. Incapable, always, of running to say, «Don't be afraid, I'm like that, nothing is going to happen to you. You have to control yourself. You're not a coward, not a sissy.» But he went on for years without saying a word except when the necessity of facing reality exploded within him, exclaiming, «Sissy, sissy! Be a man!» And little Efrén . . . Efrén . . . grew up afraid. He was comfortable only with Hermila and later, with his lifelong friend, Clemen Pereda. . . .

«But it's not his fault,» Pedro Ferrón said. He pushed the glider back in place, filled his glass again and sat down carefully.

Several minutes passed. The sky cleanly blue, the afternoon hot, heavy — from the terrace he could see the Government Palace and the tower of the Cathedral. Confused, louder, came the sound of voices, shouts, songs. Laughs, marimbas, maracas . . . He was alone, he was not going to Carnival . . . . He didn't have anywhere to go . . . No . . . Yes . . . Yes, he did have somewhere to go . . . Yes. He got up and, walking carefully, went over to the chrysanthemums. Down below, his black Packard was gleaming. He smiled. Yes, he had somewhere to go.

* * *

Daniel laughed out loud.

«But this is crazy!»

«Decide!» Jacobo demanded. «Yes or no?»

«Naturally, yes!» Daniel answered. «Of course, yes!»

Alicia was watching him. Her face lit up.

«O.K.! Then everyone says yes!»

«Right away!» Carmela clowned being in a hurry.

«First,» Hernán said, «Alicia and Carmela ought to have a double gin, so they won't get cold feet when we get there.»

«Yes, yes!» Luis said.

«And Daniel needs a double, too.»

«Two doubles,» Daniel said.

Carmela started a dance.

«The beautiful butterflies of love . . .» and she dropped to the grass.

«Leave that until after the drinks,» said Jacobo and pulled her up.

«The drinks are over there,» Alicia said, pointing toward the pool. They all ran. Daniel took her hand.

Jacobo and Carmela were in the best places. Luis threw himself on the ground, and with his face hanging over the pool, wet his head.

«Call Professor Wells!» Hernán exclaimed. «He would enjoy it!»

«And Alma?» Carmela asked.

«What an indiscreet association of ideas!» Jacobo reprimanded.

«I mean,» Carmela explained, «we ought to call Alma. We agreed to meet here.»

«Quiet!»

«No explanations!»

«We don't want any gossip!»

«Well,» Carmela protested, «if Alma and Wells are going together, I didn't know it.»

In chorus, the rest cried, «Quiet. Quiet.»

* * *

Clementina Pereda felt her heart throbbing. She came to the corner of the Plaza del Carbón and stopped in front of El Arbol. She brushed off her dress. («What a bunch of Indians!») She thought of lice, mange and sores. Fear did not make her feel any cooler. She hated all the common fiestas, the big crowds — September Fifteenth, the Twentieth of November, the Feast of the Virgin of Guadalupe, Epiphany and Carnival. She felt personally affronted by the invasion of booths in the main streets. They sold everything, everything! She blushed, deeply embarrassed, not so much by the purple panties and brassieres («how common . . . such a dignified, respectable color!») as by the little clay chicks. And she remembered all she knew about them — they say they look cute but when you lift the top, you see revolting, awful, obscene things inside! There's a pair of figures, a man and a woman making . . . Clemen turned red. Now that she had stopped a short distance from a booth where they were sold, she felt it was her great, anonymous chance to buy one of them . . . but an unmarried lady, a daughter of Dr. Pereda (May he rest in peace), a member of the Guild of St. Mary . . . She . . . I? . . . Never!

Clementina ran toward the Banderilla bus. No one knows me, she told herself, elbowing her way through the crowd of women. In her hurry she almost fell over the legs of a sturdy, young man and in the confusion didn't realize it until she was almost under . . . What rabble! Now they pushed against her and she felt — with delighted repugnance — the warmth of his strong legs. Legs like trees. Legs of a tough, warm man . . . The conductor said impatiently, «Ladies . . . please.»

Clemen didn't get over her embarrassment until she was seated. However, her tribulations and disgust found one consolation — there was no one she knew. The women and men around her came from some nearby ranch. No one was from Jalapa. No one knew that she, Clementina Pereda, was riding in the Banderilla bus, just to go to Sedeño. To the place where those women died . . . No one will ever know it, she told herself and in breathing her triumph also breathed in something very disagreeable. But, now that she realized it was too late to change her mind, the bus started. Ever since she was six years old, Clemen had closed her eyes when she found herself in a tight spot. She closed them. She told herself various things — I don't think anyone knows me. Nice people wouldn't be here now. If anyone sees me, I'll say I'm going to the dressmaker in Banderilla. But no one notices a second class bus. If I tell them I'm going to the dressmaker's, they will say it's because I don't want to be ostentatious, because of my Christian humility, because I can very well afford to pay for a cab and I'm not stingy. No, indeed! Not like those miserable Ferróns who only eat well when they have guests and that only twice a year! No, not me. Also we are democratic and we live in a country that has already had a revolution, it's natural to have uprisings . . . (That business about *democracy* and that we *already* have had a revolution, Don Higinio Rivadeneyra said at the last dinner meeting of the Rotary Club. She remembered it very well because she remembered everything Don Higinio said and did that night. He was impertinent, a little tight, and shamelessly dared to put his hand on her knee — under the tablecloth. What did he think? That I'm just anybody? She didn't say so to him but she gave him a pinch that instead of embarrassing him, encouraged him). And if not, they'll say I inherited it from Papá, because he was always so good and mixed with everyone. With everyone. And hardly charged anything for office calls. What a kind man! Maybe that's why I didn't get married. But who cares about getting married? . . . As for me, I'm not interested. I wasn't interested.

She opened her eyes. The bus was going by the side of the Normal School. To the left a row of soft green mountains cut off the horizon. Small mountains that seemed very close and cozy. When she was a child (years ago) she had gone with the others in her class to spend a day in the country. She had always remembered the scent of the oak and fir forest, a slope carpeted with dried needles that made her slip and laugh, or she saw the legs of her companions and remembered herself — a little girl full of laughter and happiness as big as if she had been lost forever. As if she were somewhere so far from the Cathedral that never again could anyone come to look for her and find her; no one to tell her no, not that, because she was the daughter of Dr. Pereda . . . and that . . . No, that was not true. She had never been restricted by her father. Just the opposite. Many times he had said he wanted her to marry, that he wanted grandchildren. But she was the one it bothered. She imagined her pregnancy — the nausea, the increasing size of her abdomen, the whims and later the pain — and she knew her father would take care of her, as he did for all the important women in town. And then, no . . . for Papá to see me . . . no, never . . . better to be an old maid! Anyway, I was always dull, because my friends, even the ones with no personality . . .

Clementina blinked. It was a gorgeous afternoon. I'm remembering all those things to keep from thinking about what I'm going to do, she told herself, and her heart beat fast. Then she added, bad or not, I want to do it. I'll confess it.

The bus was rapidly approaching the bridge. Clemen pulled on the cord to stop it. She got up hastily and, stumbling, fell into the hands of the robust young man who deposited her (almost lifted her) on the ground.

Clementina never had sinned. Her wanting to go to the bridge at Sedeño was bad. She already knew it. But . . . the ground sank.

I, Clementina, who hates big crowds, what have I come to!

And, terrified, she saw a woman («A nobody, you can see it a mile off!») come toward her to sell some pictures.

«Of those poor women,» she said, sobbing, «the martyrs.»

Frightened, Clemen bought all four.

*　*　*

Daniel thought, This is why I like Jalapa. Only the people in Jalapa do this. Alicia pinched him but he didn't notice. Eulogize the prostitutes, eulogize the degenerate.

«They're going to kill you!» Jacobo said smiling.

«They will lynch you! They will lynch you!» Carmela cried in cha-cha-cha rhythm. «They will stab you twenty times, you and Alicia! Boom-boom-boom! Cha-cha-cha!»

Luis tried to follow her steps and fell on the ground.

«More respect! More respect! It's a day of mourning!» a drunk said, standing by rigidly, a statue with round, bloodshot eyes.

The highway was blocked. The Mexico City to Veracruz and Veracruz to Mexico City buses had been forced to stop. The passengers got out and went toward the crowd. So many people! What's happening?

Borrito Garza was traveling on the bus from Mexico City to Veracruz. He lived in the capital but sometimes he needed «to leave civilization» and go to Jalapa. He said goodbye to all his friends by phone and to his new love in person, then went off to «enlighten the provinces.» He had left the «provinces» during the Thirties, when he realized his ardent sex life could not be carried to fulfillment without leading to ruin and shame for the rest of the Garzas. Borrito was aware of the dignity and importance of his family, so he sacrificed himself and decided to «put in an appearance» among his old friends only when the city got to be «just too much.»

Borrito conquered his depression and was the third one off the bus. He wasn't travelling with anybody. That was exactly why he had come to Carnival («Jalapa gets more cultured all the time. One always finds someone interesting.») and he thought that, in his honor, the festivities were starting at Sedeño.

«What . . . what?» he asked, pushing ahead.

No one paid any attention to him and he kept on, «What . . . what?»

A woman in a rebozo answered him staring at him with two large, yellowish eyes.

«Don't you know? Raimunda died, and Chona . . . and two others . . . Last . . . early this morning, they were coming from Banderilla drunk and lost their lives with the architect . . . It was his car . . . he killed them, they died with him . . . Didn't you know?»

«No, I just came from Mexico City,» explained Borrito.

«Come,» the woman said, turning into his guide, «over there. There's still blood.»

* * *

Carmela leaned against the bridge. Hernan came close to her and put his hand over hers.

«This is a romantic spot, don't you think?»

«Devastatingly,» she responded, «like you.»

«Well,» Hernán pretended to be angry, «somebody's nice to you . . .»

«I'd be nice to *you* . . . But, no!»

They clasped hands tightly. Carmela looked into his eyes.

«I don't like this,» she said.

Hernán hugged her.

«It's . . .» he answered. «It's . . . better look at the water, the rocks, the landscape.»

They came close to each other. Carmela felt Hernan's cheek, warmly damp, on her ear. For a few moments she almost felt the security of being close to some kind of fulfillment. Her eyes clouded over. The last rays of the sun slanted across the tops of the trees. The river swirled against some large rocks, disappeared from view and farther down, burst forth in foam. On the left bank some men — tied at the waist — were climbing down.

«Hey, look . . . some false teeth!»

* * *

Don Pedro Ferrón finally went to the side and let some other curiosity seekers take his place.

«The car was demolished!» he commented. «And the latest model!»

«Man, it was a beautiful car!» Don Higinio said.

«And brand new!» Don Pablo exclaimed.

«Terrible luck!» Don Pedro said and started to walk along with the others.

«No one crosses this line,» Don Higinio declared. «No one.»

They walked peacefully, as if they were on Calle Real or in Parque Juárez.

«Look, look!» Don Pablo said suddenly, taking off his hat. «All the Rotarians!»

«That's fine,» Don Pedro exclaimed, greeting the president. «Here we all are. No one can criticize anyone else.»

«Well, if we're all here, there's nothing wrong in it.»

«Of course not.»

«Look, look!» Don Pedro cried again, more excited. «The Lions, too!»

* * *

«Clementina!» Borrito exclaimed.

«Borrito!» Clementina exclaimed.

«What a miserably hot day!» Borrito said, raising his hand to his heart. «To be entertained by this spectacle. I am here accidentally. I was coming from Mexico City and they stopped the bus.»

«I was going to Banderilla! To the dressmaker's . . . But they stopped me, too.»

Both had photographs in their hands. Clemen explained, «They say the money is for candles.»

«They told me it was for the funeral. . .»

* * *

Seated on a rock, Alicia and Daniel were watching the river.

«Mamá is worse than ever now,» Daniel said. «The divorce has her beside herself.»

«It must be difficult,» she said.

«Sometimes I feel like going to see him and getting everything patched up.»

«But could it be patched up?»

No . . . no, I don't think so.»

They embraced.

* * *

Tino handed her a cup of coffee. Adriana slipped off her shoes and propped her feet up on the sofa.

«What are they like?» she asked.

«You'll see, you'll see,» Tino said sitting next to her. «After your first impression, I'll tell you who is who . . . But don't worry, they're not clods!»

The door bell rang.

«Our bell?» she asked.

«Guests,» Tino answered and with his shoes off too, got up to answer the door.

Adriana didn't move. She heard voices — soon I will know who they are, I'll be part of the group . . . we will live here . . . Jalapa will be our home . . . everything will be all right and Mamá will come to see us every month and . . .

Tino came in with a couple — he, very thin, smiling, well dressed. She pretty, very young . . .

«Professor Wells . . . Alma Rincón . . . Our first guests!»

* * *

Sara and Barbara stepped back to look at the table.

Juice dripped from the skin of the turkey and came all the way up to the lettuce leaves edging the platter. Canapes of tuna, cheese, cucumbers, anchovies, bowls with asparagus, artichoke hearts, black olives, mushrooms, seafood salad and pistachio *flan*. The decoration was of violets covering the candlestick bases.

Leandro entered tying his tie.

«Am I O.K.?» he asked.

«Gorgeous!» Barbara said taking off her apron. «Handsomer than Rock Hudson.»

«At his best,» Sara finished.

And Sara believed it. Every time she said how handsome her husband was her face lit up. Sara was pretty too, but she always thought her sister was prettier — Barbara is really beautiful. Everything looks right on Barbara. She is so lovely . . . The Garcés sisters — born scarcely ten months apart — grew up always together. They went to kindergarten the same year and from then on everything was the same for both — «They are like twins.» It flattered them to be twins and they didn't deny it. Sara, the older, never thought praise of Barbara could be slighting of her. Just the opposite. The nice things said about Barbara seemed to have no limit and, at the same time, to include her. Besides, there was a sentence, often repeated, that convinced her of this. «My Barbara, no, no, I mean my Sara . . . well, you have different names for everyone else, but for me you are the same. I adore you both. You are equally beautiful and sweet.» Papá used to say it and his actions never belied it. The motherless Sara and Barbara enjoyed the same pampering from Don Javier — Papá-Mamá — always concerned about their sicknesses, their new clothes, their school grades and their friends. It was Papá who brought Bartolomé home one day. Two years after that visit Barbara and Bartolomé were married. Some months later Don Javier called Sara on the phone, «You are so strong, so independent . . . You, you are like me! . . . I mean you understand me. You will understand me. . . I want to get married, too.» And Sara, who *understood* better than Barbara, was maid of honor. Don Javier married a girl from Uruguay — twenty-one years old — and went with her to Montevideo. Sara stayed by herself in Mexico City. Then, one day, a letter from Bartolomé . . . «and Barbara and I want you to come to Jalapa to live with us. At least try it. If you don't like it, you can go back.» But she did like it. She liked Leandro Montes. And, curiously, from the beginning the satisfaction of being with him was like the satisfaction of growing up with Barbara. Leandro got the same kind of attention, admiration and spoiling that Barbara had received and, as usual, Sara felt all the pleasantries included her and she enjoyed them more than the recipient. Don Javier Garcés sent his consent and blessing by certified air mail and explained, «Virginia and I will not be able to come. She is a bit delicate. It seems you will soon have a small brother or sister. . .» Sara, enchanted, commented, «Oh, I hope it will be a brother. That's what Papá needs.» The wedding of Leandro Montes (in Jalapa they couldn't think of «the wedding of Sara Garcés») turned out to be very pretty. Sara was radiant during the ceremony and reception. And she still was, two years later.

«Is my tie all right?» Leandro asked.

It was his way of saying he hoped Sara would fix it. She did and he gave her a kiss on the cheek.

«Go ahead and kiss all you want,» Barbara said going out. «I'm going to call Bartolomé. It's time for him to be here.» If his hangover is better, she said to herself.

She went into the living room, sat down in a chair and dialed the number. At the third ring his voice said «Yes?»

«I'm waiting for you.»

«Yes,» Bartolomé said sarcastically, «and your children, too! I've been nursemaid for more than two hours. You must have thought I was going to sleep the whole afternoon and sober up. But no! Neither one or the other! I couldn't sleep and, in order to endure your children, I had to have a couple of drinks.»

Six, at least, Barbara thought, and said, «And how are they now?» speaking very sweetly. Bartolomé had advised her to do so. «If you see I'm furious, or if you notice I've had too much to drink, don't cross me or do anything to exasperate me, it's best. . .» Bartolomé knew himself very well; the formula worked. He responded quietly, «They're asleep already . . . I'll come in a minute. I won't be long. . .»

«Love you,» she said.

«Love you,» he replied.

* * *

When Bartolomé entered Leandro's house, the room was full. There were about forty people counting faculty members, students and friends of Leandro. He smiled at Clementina Pereda. Professor Arnaldo Wells came toward him.

«Come here,» Arnaldo demanded, taking him by the hand.

«I called you about twenty times this morning,» Bartolomé said in a low voice, letting himself be led along.

Arnaldo Wells didn't hear him. He pulled him until he was in front of Borrito Garza.

«Since you're from Jalapa,» Arnaldo said, without letting go his hand, «you will decide it. Because, in the first place, this gentlemen,» he pointed toward Borrito, «doesn't want to admit I'm right, though I assume it's only a case of cretinism and, in short, he doesn't know the meaning of the terms.» Arnaldo breathed noisily and continued the battle. «He says there is no oligarchy in Mexico. . . right?»

Borrito stood up and embraced Bartolomé. Bartolomé felt Borrito's warm, moist cheek rest on his own briefly, discreetly but insistently. Borrito was sweating. Bartolomé didn't want to take out his handkerchief. Borrito took him by the other hand (Arnaldo hadn't yet let go) and said, «In my opinion this gentleman, in addition to suffering from a cretinism worse than mine, is ill mannered. But with this difference clarified, given this explanation which seems more necessary because he is pulling you around so you can settle an argument you haven't heard a word of, given this explanation, I repeat that in Mexico there is no oligarchy. And, if this gentleman,» pointing to Arnaldo, «had listened to me, he would know that I, after the assertion repeated so many times, I added that there is no oligarchy but a monarchy. That we are to-day worse off than before! That, thanks to the PRI, the doctrine of 'three different persons and one true God,' in our country has been converted into three hundred, three thousand or whatever you like! And one true God. Taking turns, but only one . . .»

The emphatic explanation of Borrito, who took on as a personal problem anything under discussion, made Bartolomé burst into laughter. Arnaldo also laughed.

«Oh! Oh, excuse me!» Arnaldo said, giving Borrito an *abrazo*. «I'm really a little tight . . . I didn't hear you exactly. I swear . . .»

Alma's green eyes gazed lovingly at Professor Wells.

«You're seeing him with a halo shining over his bald spot,» Bartolomé said sitting down next to her.

Alma didn't move her eyes. She answered, «I like him a lot. I love him.»

* * *

«Bartolomé shouldn't be so familiar with his students.»

«Forget it,» Sara exclaimed. «Don't turn into a nag!»

Barbara put her hand to her throat.

«Besides,» Sara continued, «you know this child, Alma, is going to marry Wells.»

«I'm not thinking about Alma,» Barbara answered, lighting a cigarette, «but about Alicia, and that Carmela . . . and all the others.»

Sara looked at her steadily. She took her hand and said, «Don't be silly. Bartolomé is true to you. You can be sure. And if you think otherwise, whatever happens will be your own fault.»

«I never blame my faults on anyone else,» she answered quickly and thought, Idiot! Leandro will be unfaithful to you. Immediately she was sorry and squeezed Sara's hand. She said, «You are much better than I am . . . You are . . . good.»

* * *

Alicia put on her *capuchon*. She looked at herself in the mirror. Her eyes hardly visible through the scratchy slits in the black cloth. She smiled and felt afraid. Her eyes (hardly visible) told her nothing. In front of the mirror nothing changed. Carmela and Margarita already had their masks on.

«I think it's too much,» Alicia said. «I think we ought not to go . . . it's a lack of respect . . . I don't know!»

Carmela and Margarita took her by the hand and made her run downstairs.

39

At the foot of the steps the men, also masked, waited.

«Something to numb the conscience,» Jacobo said offering them a tray of cocktails. «I prepared it special.»

Alicia drank hers in one gulp. It was not the first time she had been drunk, but it was the first time she did it intentionally. She thought about it and it seemed appropriate in the middle of this enormous room («the entrance hall» as her mother said so proudly) that had always seemed false to Alicia. Anyway, she told herself, it's what people expect of the young mistress of all this . . .

Daniel came over and put his arm around her shoulders.

«Give your car keys to Jacobo,» he said, «You're coming with me.»

«I'll take Margarita,» Luis Rentería said.

* * *

Sara returned with the empty tray. She put it on the kitchen table and sat down with Clementina.

«You are the only one who can understand me,» Clemen said with happy eyes — her pupils dilated, shining. «Ha ha! It was only a joke . . . But it just came to me! . . . Please don't tell Leandro! Imagine his aunt doing such things! . . Ha ha!» Clementina glowed. «But everyone in Jalapa was there . . . Not very many saw me, but I saw everybody. Borrito saw me, but he's like one of the family . . . I, myself, have sworn to go to Confession early tomorrow and then take Communion. And the rest of Lent no one will see hair nor hide of me . . . I'm going to go into seclusion in my own house. Efrén, I mean Father Ferrón, says that is the most sensible thing, that I don't have to go to those vulgar Retreats they have now where you can drink coca-cola and even, if you're feeling ill or weak, a little brandy . . . He says it's preferable, if you do it with conviction and faith, to retreat within yourself — to take your own house for a jail, well, no not a jail, but a cell, a religious cell, of course. That it has lots of advantages. Today . . . Oh, dear. Ha ha! I went out with him and his mother after dinner and, I don't know, the demon alcohol or Satan made me lie and say I had a headache and better go home . . . but I'm just an awful liar. I went out to the highway toward Revolucion to the Banderilla buses . . . but I swear . . .»

It was the nth time that Clemen had told about her adventure. Clementina, at forty-eight, laughed and moved with the clumsiness and flirtatiousness of a thirteen-year-old girl. Of course, without the same effect, or really without any effect.

Bartolomé and Barbara, arms tightly interlaced, came into the kitchen.

«Oh!» Clemen exclaimed. «Don't tell them!»

* * *

«I think I'm drunk,» Arnaldo Wells said.

«But you look very nice that way,» Alma whispered to him.

* * *

Alicia sat with her head on Daniel's shoulder. They had arrived. The lights of the car went out and for a few seconds she had the sensation of falling in the absolute darkness. She felt Daniels's hand on her leg. He caressed her, softly and murmured, explaining, excusing himself:

«You wanted to come.»

They got out of the car.

Ever since she was nine or ten, Alicia had known what kind of house this was. A place they talked about in low tones. A place that her friends at Motolinía School used to describe with extravagant gestures. A place she had found while riding around the city with her parents (in the security — almost like home — of Papá's enormous automobile) and whose exact location she had confirmed by the looks, gestures and changes in her parents' attitudes. Now she was here. She had dreamed often of being here. But she hadn't dreamed about the fear that made her tremble, or the mud, or the darkness that kept her from seeing, or about hearing a Litany. The Rosary.

She and Daniel were the last of the group.

«We ought not to go in,» she begged. «I don't think they will like it.»

But Margarita and Carmela had already returned, masked, excited.

«There are lots of disguises! Don't worry!»

Daniel, mechanically, had followed the prayer. He thought of Father Ferrón and felt an immense shame. «You will fall down and down,» his mother said, «and when you realize it, it will be because the mire is already up to your knees. Just like your father.» And Daniel, who always laughed to hear her say it, remembered it now and it seemed prophetic to him. He, here, he who never. . . he who, yes, was a virgin, coming here, with his girl! But he took one step after another.

«Yes, yes!» he exclaimed with exaggeration. «Don't pay any attention, no one is going to recognize you! Let's go.»

Alicia, her hand clutching his arm firmly, her face covered by the hood, said immediately, «Yes, I will go.»

And she was on her way, walking rapidly. Sliding in the mud, she came to the two cement steps. She looked up. Some crepe paper streamers, faded, full of cobwebs. She looked down and was already in the room — women and men seated, drinking something, smoking. The tables ringed the dance floor, almost covered by the four coffins.

Never, ever, would anyone imagine it! Daniel was exclaiming inwardly, becoming more and more euphoric. I was always afraid; and now here I am, so calm. . . And with Alicia. If she only knew! But no one knows. . . Daniel felt a tear slip out and moved closer to Alicia, felt her soft, warm, yielding. . . He bit her hair through the hood of her costume. Alicia felt it. She turned her head toward him waiting for another bite. Daniel felt complete, strong, virile for the first time. And so he was. His body was awakening, indomitable, liberated. . . And here! In this place it was permitted, demanded! But no. . . there was no requirement, just like a normal thing. . . And he, also normal, was here and full of desire, great desire. He, erect, was the best proof, the definitive proof.

* * *

«One was called Raimunda, another Sandra, another Lola, and the other Chona. Here they are . . .» Margarita pointed them out on the photograph.

«This is brutal,» she exclaimed in a low tone. «When I write to my friends in Mexico City, they're not going to believe me. They'll say it's pure fiction, that I ought to write a story . . . Who would have said we'd be here, masked, in a brothel? At a wake! It's pure Kafka!»

«More likely Faulkner — *Sanctuary*.»

«Well, yes,» Margarita agreed, «but there's a certain feeling . . . an atmosphere.» Suddenly she cried, «Neither Faulkner nor Kafka. It's authentic Mexican! Mexicanism it really is!»

Jacobo nudged Hernán.

«She's from the big city!»

«And why not 'Jalapeño it really is'?»

«Yes, why not?» Hernán said.

«*Mexicanism it really is, Salvadorean it really is, Guatemalan it really is, Costa Rican it really is.*»

«*Guatemalan, guatemalteco, guatemaltico . . . Tico tico no fuba. . .* Carmela sang.

Everyone laughed.

Compact, whispering groups filled the big room. The coffins seemed almost to be merged into one — enormous — by the accumulation of all the wreaths and sprays of flowers. Spiked coffee and cuba-libres were served free; if anyone wanted something else, he could buy it by the bottle.

«Tonight is no time to be cheap,» Popotes, the madam, said. «That we don't need!»

A whisper, growing stronger, less a whisper, started moving from one group to another, round the room, grew louder, until finally it reached Popotes, and she agreed.

«Yes, yes! They would like it! Let's have some music!»

And the music started — very respectful, almost liturgical. Someone played a guitar and another sang. Their identities were whispered from group to group — «The blonde boy playing the guitar is Chona's brother and the singer, in the blue pants, is, was, Sandra's husband . . .»

Everyone drank quietly and quickly. The other girls, sighing, continued aloud the prayers for their companions. Mascara streaked by tears, cigarettes smoked to the last drag, drinks swallowed at one gulp, everything has a special quality tonight — in honor of them. It is for them.

Popotes didn't put any limit on the drinks, saying, «It doesn't matter how much we spend tonight. Carnival starts tomorrow and we'll make up for it . . . Anyway it's worth it for Lola. She was the dean here, and the most respected.»

«Yes, indeed, no one was better than she was.»

«Let's drink to her!»

They drank. Then someone shouted,

«And to Chona, also.» A man in a well-cut black suit, in mourning, almost weeping, with a bottle of tequila in his hand, «She was the best of the best, and anybody who doesn't think so is a m.... To her health!»

Everyone drank with him.

«And for Sandra!» another in black.

«And for Raimunda, what the hell!»

«For all of them!»

«The four of them!»

«And the architect, too!» Onésima said, the only one who remembered him.

«Yes, for him, too!»

«Bring more cuba-libres, Micaela!» Onésima called.

Micaela was the queer who waited on the tables. He ran eagerly to obey.

«Let's go,» Alicia begged Daniel. She felt sick.

Carmela grabbed Jacobo's arm and begged, «Let's go. . . let's go.»

Daniel and Hernán dragged Jacobo out.

Even in their cars, they could still hear the last lines sung by Sandra's husband and the other man.

It was a little red house
and they made it look new
with the life blood of Rosita
that's how they touched it up
that's how they touched it up.

*   *   *

43

Father Efrén woke up sweating, frightened. The same dream again: he, Leandro, and Bartolomé, once again, children in school. Again Leandro — a beautiful child — teasing him. Now he knew without doubt he hated him. . . It's because I saw him yesterday, he said to himself. He pressed his fingers on his temples, then got up and knelt on the cold flagstones. But he was trembling and hot. Trembling, he was too conscious of his body.

Horrified he bit his lips. . .

*　*　*

It's because of the fiesta. . . I mean, the drinking. . . I mean, I am sorry not to have known you before. I assure you, I had prepared a welcome speech, but now, at this hour, and in this condition, only . . . I am so glad you are here! . . We love Tino and we love you, too!»

«Thank you, you are very kind.»

«Bravo,» Borrito cried. «I love spontaneous speeches!»

In the kitchen Barbara said to Sara, «Now he's making a speech!»

«To whom?»

«To Adriana, Tino's wife.»

«Stop it! Don't pay any attention! Everyone has drunk more than he should, even Clementina. At least she's already gone.»

They stopped talking and kept on eating *flan*.

Suddenly, very clearly, they heard weeping. Both stopped eating. They heard, in confusion, the noise from the living room, but although very weak, the other sound grew. . . became especially noticeable.

Carefully Sara opened the back door. Now the crying could be heard clearly.

Sara stepped into the darkness.

«Who. . . who is crying?»

Victoria dried her eyes with her apron.

«I am. . . señora.»

«But Victoria!»

«What's wrong?» Barbara asked, behind her.

«I felt like crying.» Victoria explained.

«Did something happen to you?» Barbara asked. «Has anyone done anything to you?»

«No, señora, no. . . I just wanted to cry.»

«Do you like to cry?» Barbara asked.

«Yes, señora, I like to.»

«Leave her alone.» Sara said. And to the maid, «Go to bed, Victoria. It's very late.»

«Yes, señora. I'm going to bed now.»

* * *

«Not I,» Alicia said, her face flaming.

«Not me either,» Carmela said. «We'll stay here. It's already late.»

«But we're invited,» Hernán repeated.

«But not at this hour,» Alicia said.

«But it's hardly one o'clock!» Luis Rentería said.

«Hardly!» Carmela repeated. «Good night!»

«Well, I'm going,» Margarita said. «I'm used to Mexico City. On Saturday night, at this hour!»

¯«Stop bragging! I'd bet you're a virgin.»

«Imbecile! Margarita protested. «That would be my mistake!»

«Well,» Hernán said, «let's take the little girl from the big city to Maestro Montes' party.»

«Let's go!» Daniel shouted.

«She's going to corrupt us!» Jacobo exclaimed.

«Please,» Alicia begged, «go on!»

* * *

Daniel stopped the car abruptly in front of Leandro's house.

«You and Batuta get more and more like each other every day,» Jacobo said.

«Rich kids,» Hernán shouted. «The obvious product of capitalism.»

«Well, I think it really is rather late,» Margarita said. «I live near here. I can walk.»

«Wait,» Luis said. «I'll go with you.»

* * *

Zenaida López, queen of the Carnival, was one of the first to wake up that Sunday. Well, no, she wasn't queen of the Carnival, but she was queen. I really am, by far! Jalapa had named Lina queen of the Carnival, but . . . but. . . Everyone says so. People who live here and strangers, too, are convinced: Zenaida will be the queen. . . And she imagines what they are thinking when they decide she will be queen, and not Lina: She will be darling in those spangled see-throughs. . . with that beautiful body. . . and she's so young. . . and so lovely. . . No! Zenaida is queen no matter what they say. . . She really is!

(She heard applause.)

Zenaida is a million times more beautiful than Lina.

Zenaida is a dish.

45

She's tops. None better.

Silvina Pinal and Elsa Aguirre will be small potatoes.

Yes, she will beat them all, even Félix, if she comes. . .

Everyone!

Pinal will ride in the Dos Equis float, and Aguirre in Carta Blanca's. . . but Jalapa can show the whole world what Jalapa's women are like with. . . Zenaida!

Maria Félix is a deluxe edition.

And that's a compliment to Maria.

Well, of course, because Zenaida is something special, beautiful and (Zenaida blushes in her bed and hears more applause so she almost wants — because of the rhythm and uniforms — to go back to sleep. She closes her eyes and keeps on:)

Respected by all.

Of course! I swear it!

She is a saint.

Zenaida is a virgin.

Of course, she is better than anyone, naturally. . . she's very much a homebody, she loves her parents, she works hard, she's well mannered, she's friendly to everyone. . . There's no one like her!

Well, yes, I can't deny that, but they say she's going around with Genaro Almanza. . . Yes! I'm not kidding! They say the two of them are very buddy-buddy.

Sixty-six thousand voices cry, «No!».

(Zenaida squirms, she curls up, sighs, doubts, feels drowsy, wants to sleep, wants to keep on thinking about Zenaida. . . She yawns and continues:)

That's the way it always is. You no sooner have a beautiful girl than they immediately start to malign her.

(Zenaida decides they said the same thing about Maria Félix; it's still early; she goes back to sleep, and she snores, lightly, but she snores).

* * *

Clementina made her confession to Father Loyo («He's so good!» «He doesn't even seem like a Jesuit!» «I always thought he would die before Papá, but no, God keeps him here for us. . . like a piece of parchment . . . pure spirit») and Father Ferrón («How pale he is!» «How he shakes!») gave her Communion. A strange day; a vacuum full of palpitations, omens, and fears. Clemen returned to her pew. She didn't pray at all. With her head bowed, she looked at the marble, obscene marble that made her think of dirty things she didn't dare tell even to her confessor. Because after I tell it he will come to sit in my pew and say I have a dirty mind, that the figures I see don't exist, that it

is my evil nature, my sins. . . no, that I won't even tell God the Father!
No, no, no! Clementina prayed to himself. I shouldn't be evil minded so
soon after Communion! No, my God, don't let me! All the parties will be
spoiled and there will be fog all day and all night. . . It's going to be cold and
the people out on the town looking for fun and temptation will be disap-
pointed. Yes, indeed, Thanks to the Lord. It's going to rain. . .
Clemetina was saying it all in a very low tone. She seemed to be praying. .

* * *

Daniel stopped the car at the door of his house. He sat rigidly for a long
time, then suddenly heard the bells of the cathedral. Daniel shook his head as
if with the movement he could avoid or drive away the sound. . . Better not to
think. . . Not to think of anything. Not to be himself. Not to have to be
himself. Nor to have a mother. . . a father, well, Papá isn't here! . .
Shakespeare: To be or not to be. He: To desire or not to desire. To desire and
repent immediately. Not to desire and to worry. But yes, in a kind of fog there
came to his mind the knowledge, the memory. Yes, I can. I really can. Yes. . .
What a fool! There's a different yes and no for everyone. For me, yes. . . He
blinked. The street, paved with stones, shone quiet and wet. I'll never forget
this Jalapa — this street, this silence of bells and birds. This mixed-up night of
harmless drunks. . . These stones starting to shine, maybe from sun, maybe
from rain. The light and water mix, at times appearing the same. And I, cold
and stupid, stay here, stuck to the steering wheel, putting on an act, playing a
drunk. . . Maybe I know that going in is less honest and even if I spend the
night there, even if nothing unusual happens, I cannot see her or accept (and if
I see her and accept her) and maybe what bothers me is Papá. . . and yet. . .
Everything is so. . .
In his lower belly he felt the warming again. He opened his fly and looked
at himself.
«This has been, but no more.»
The glass door opened. The maid — freshly combed — appeared, shivering. She smiled on realizing she had been right.
«I thought it was you.»
Daniel started the car. He smiled vaguely. He thought: I'm still going in. . .
it doesn't matter that. . . He pushed in the clutch, shifted into first, and stepped on the accelerator harder and harder, and to the surprise of the maid,
turned the corner and went down the street. Soon he was in the main street; he
crossed it at high speed; it was raining and people were coming out of early
mass, but he didn't see anyone; he continued beside Juárez Park and went
rapidly down Ursulo Galván street.

* * *

Onésima knew lots of men and was a little tired of them, but was always grateful to Daniel for that night. Well, not night any longer, it was the Sunday of Carnival and Onésima, who had gone to bed with lots of men, and who knew all of them, said to herself, «I'll never know anyone else like this in my whole life. . .»

And Daniel, also, was content.

* * *

Borrito couldn't sleep. He lit a cigarette, being careful not to let the ashes fall on the rug. He yawned.

«I'm plastered.»

The phone rang. He looked at his watch — quarter past eight.

«Only Clementina could call me at this hour,» he said aloud, walking toward the phone. «Hello?»

It was Clementina.

* * *

Ana opened her eyes: it was still fairly dark. Rain was hitting against the window panes — hidden behind the curtains. The atmosphere was grey and sad. Ana felt afraid and shrank down in the bedclothes. She heard Maria walking in the television room and cried, «Maria!»

The door opened immediately. Maria asked, «Awake already?»

«Bring me the cat. I want him here with me.»

Maria smiled.

«You dreamt about him. Just a minute, let me see if he's out on the town.»

Maria closed the door. There she was again in that gloomy light, in the rain and silence and solitude. Only the warmth of the bed comforted her. It was nice. She snuggled down in the bed again and shut her eyes tightly. A few moments this way and then she opened them again — now her bedroom seemed large and empty. Her clothes from yesterday were on the big chair, her shoes on the rug near the rubber toys. Papá had said, «You have to pick them up before you go to bed,» but she still hadn't picked them up. She closed her eyes to keep from looking at them. She turned over and opened her eyes again. Her grandmother's picture. . . «she's so nice. . .» Nothing else on the wall. Only the door where Maria comes in with the cat.

«He loves you, too! Here he is!»

Ana started stroking him and fell asleep again. Much later she wakened because he was rubbing against her cheek. Ana pulled back. She heard her parents' voices, far away but clear.

«You must do it for your children.» — (Mamá).

«I said for myself and I forgive your stupidity.» — (Papá).

Ana opened her door and met Toni, also awake. They looked at each other happily and joined hands. She ran faster than he, almost pulling him by the time they got to their parents' room.

«Bonjour,» Bartolomé said.

«Why so early?» Barbara asked.

But soon she heard noises from the street, Maria's footsteps, the paper boy's cry and vague, but recognizable, the voices of the women who lived on the block.

«It's after seven,» Barbara said putting on her robe.

«After seven-thirty,» Bartolomé said. «We have marvelous children.»

«Yes, of course! So you're going to stay in bed!»

«Well, I meant to say 'children and wife.' And I'm going to sleep and sleep and

«Sleep. . . I know. Go back to sleep!»

*　*　*

At times there is a vague, blurred noise — some footsteps. Someone who runs and exists only in the imagination. Then a silence. Then, later, much later, something that confirms the running and the exactness of the hour and your condition. But no. If you close your eyes, you can fall asleep again. The rest is ominous. It's a conspiracy so you can't sleep. . . But not everything. . . There is an ancient, monotonous sound that is an invitation to go back to sleep. Yes. It's not late. Or if it is, there's nothing to lose. Go to sleep. . . it's raining. . . yes, it's raining hard. Now the sound of the big drops on the roofs is very clear — the water running through the gutters, occasionally trapped, languid, mute, and suddenly falling drop by drop on the paving stones in the gallery. Yes, it's raining. I'm going to sleep. All Jalapa will be soaked.

Hernán put his head under the pillow. His body stretched out over the bed. Alone. Vastly alone.

Vastly alone he opened his eyes and thought of Carmela. He remembered the afternoon, her cheek, the river, the dead prostitutes, the wake, the party, confused, blurred, aggressive (I was going to fight with someone I don't remember who) at Professor's Montes' house. He remembered Sara said, «Drink this coffee, Hernán. Drink it. You'll feel better.» And Hernán didn't want to feel better; that is, he didn't want to feel different: he felt fine, but he took the coffee because of her kindness, her face, her sweetness.

The rain was not imagined. It messed up Carnival. As always in Jalapa!

All we have left is the Emir. Thousands of people in one single place. . . And Hernán slept again.

* * *

«You lied,» Luis Rentería said.

«Don't talk,» Margarita begged in a very low voice. She caressed Luis' bare breast, laced her fingers in the hairs growing around his nipples. «Don't say anything. . . I don't want this to end.»

«Margarita.»

«Don't talk.»

«*My* Margarita.»

«Luis. . . please. . . Luis.»

He stretched out his arm to get cigarettes, matches and lit one. Margarita's chestnut hair gleamed for a moment. He blew out the match. Once again half-light, almost dark. Margarita nibbled his chest and he bit her hair, inhaled deeply and was left with the moist, bitter aftertaste. Something new. Luis thought of Rodin. He would have liked them — above all himself — to be as beautiful as the models in «The Kiss.» There was between them in this moment something of the voluptuous chill of the bronze, something statuesque, grandiose, imperishable, and, at the same time, inexorably changeable, as ephemeral as breathing smoke in and out. To be aware of his dry mouth — dead, false. To be aware. Not to be any longer what he was a moment before. Not to be becoming. Nothing. To be no one. To be less than a statue. To feel at the moment, at any given moment, that one can achieve anything — can be wise, strong, heroic, eternal. To feel and to know — nothing. Luis put the cigarette between his lips and then slowly, deliberately, put one hand on her hair and the other on her breast — tender, firm, small. Without caressing her, placed there only to make himself an ally and part of her warmth and heartbeat. Margarita snuggled closer against his shoulder and a warm tear slid down his chest to join her fingers in the hair around his nipples, momentarily wet, immediately kissed by her. Silly. False. I have cried too often. Also he was crying again without her knowing it. To everyone his own weeping, like separate bodies.

He was afraid of the immobility and the threat of time, but he stayed still. Rodin. This moment. Rodin. A statue. Margarita and I. I. . . I. . . As if Margarita could guess it, she lowered her hand toward him, touched him, *her* him. . . *her* me. . . me that she touches caresses. Me. I. Margarita.

The moved slowly and surely until they found each other's lips again, in the closest warmth, in the saliva again separated by teeth on teeth, together again, always together.

«Kiss me, kiss me, kiss me!»

Below the new bodies helped by fingers finding each other. New. Again. Then like the desolation that walks, runs, finishes, the noises became apparent. The noises — so clear — of the city, the street, below, already in motion, and it's raining and we belong to a world. We belong here. To stop one's own throb and listen to someone else's — a little girl (by the laugh it must be a little girl) running down the steps. A noisy car. The exhaust open. More noise. A mother who screams something and breaks the spell of being in another world. The astute church that sounds its bells. Time for Mass. The city. We have (they have) awakened in Jalapa. Sunday.

«Will they say anything at your house?»

«In Jalapa I have no house,» she murmured.

«I will be your house.»

«You. . . yes. . . you.»

They caressed each other quietly — to learn to know each other by touch.

«It's trite, isn't it?» Luis asked.

«What?»

«To make the ephemeral last.»

«Nothing is trite, Luis. Nothing. I love you.»

«Margarita. We are in Jalapa. . .»

«We live in Jalapa, Luis. . . We live. . . Yes! . . . we live!»

* * *

Margarita and Luis sleep in each other's arms. Hernán Lovillo sleeps alone, snoring. Alicia and Carmela open their eyes — only to sleep again. Daniel and Onésima embrace once more and start once more. Jacobo walks down the main street, looks at the clock on La Perla — eight-thirty in the morning; he is drenched, he tries to light a cigarette that comes apart before he can get the flame up to it. The cars go by rapidly, splashing him. Zenaida López, furious, looks out at the rain from the window of her room. Bartolomé can't delay any longer. He puts on his slippers and goes down to breakfast with the children — Ana and Toni applaud. Borrito is in the shower. Clemen takes a sip of her coffee and shivers, «Madness! But I'll do it!» Sara contemplates the living room for a moment and then turns to Victoria, «Come help me.» Don Pedro Ferrón carefully opens his bedroom door, walks barefooted to the bottom of the stairs. For a few moments he is afraid the sound of the rain will prevent his knowing whether there is any danger. His heart beats rapidly. Below, Renata, their servant for ten years, appears in the doorway between the dining room and kitchen. They see each other. Renata opens the door all the way without saying a word. It's the signal every Sunday. «If I weren't the mayor, I wouldn't have the obligation,» Genaro Almanza says. Eugenia laughs, «Tell it to someone else. That Zenaida is in the business.» Alma Rincón looks at the clock. Eight-thirty. In exactly twelve more hours she will be with Arnaldo Wells. Adriana begs again, «Tino, we have to fix up the house. . . Wake up.»

* * *

At twelve o'clock the rain stopped and, like magic, one moment later Calle Real was filled with people. The first to come out were the trinket venders, eager, reconciled with the world, instantly ready to make a sale. Their agile fingers untied the knots of the plastic covers that protected the merchandise, and the water caught in them fell quietly to the sidewalk. A grey sky on the point of being cleared by the sun's rays spread a timid light over the city. As a red-ochre iridescence rose from the tile roofs, thrushes and sparrows cut through the warm, misty vapor. Singing and chirping, they gave notice that the sky was clear. Children came out on the balconies. Their arms and bodies wiped the dampness from the railings. They looked up and down the streets searching for someone in a mask, or something that showed it was Carnival time and also meant the storm was over. But the happy sign did not appear and they had to be satisfied with laughing, hoping, quickly running outside. «Come on, come on, let's go down in the street.»

And Calle Real received everyone with its costume jewelry — the envy of children and servants — cardboard masks smelling strongly of glue, Guerrero pottery, chocolate cups from Michoacan, ribbons, rebozos, puppets, dolls: primitive, strange survivors in a plastic world, made of rags and sawdust, delightfully ugly, defeated, anachronistic. The others enjoy glory and popularity — those made with the newest material and decorated in the latest style, next to the latest model cars and planes, also of plastic.

Victoria, eternally surprised, stood on the balcony, looking wide-eyed and smiling at the happy turmoil in the street below. Victoria's expression was both pleased and lonely. All her emotion seemed contained in the depths of her spirit, or of the past; and caught up in herself, she seemed so removed from the outside world that her luminous smile looked incongruous beneath her empty eyes. Victoria thought about watching the fireworks at night from this same balcony — that miracle of fire and brilliance whose magic could never be explained. Ever since she came to work for Señora Sara she'd been able to enjoy the parades and fireworks as much as she liked. . . and without any danger. . . the ever present danger of the street, the fear of getting lost, the fear of forgetting which streets were which and how they run into each other, the fear of forgetting Señora Sara's name. . . «Sara, Sara and Señor Leandro, Señor Leandro Montes.» Or the danger of losing her strength and being defenseless, unable to move, unable to run away, because you always have to run away. Or you might be mistaken for someone else; there are so many people who look alike, this could happen some day and right away she wouldn't be herself, Victoria, any more, but someone else. The solution was never to go out by herself. . . In any case, from here, although alone, she could enjoy almost everything, peacefully, without being afraid.

«Victoria!»

Below Ana and Toni, accompanied by Maria, were calling her.

«Come with us. . . Come on!»

«Come on down!»

Victoria burst out laughing. She ran inside to find Señora Sara.

«Señora Barbara's children are downstairs,» she said, still laughing, «and they want me to go with them.»

«All right. . . run along. I'll look at all of you from the balcony.»

«Aunt Sara! Can Victoria come?»

Their voices were scarcely audible. They were agreeing with each other, and continued talking about something that couldn't be understood. Victoria appeared and kissed them both. Then Ana took her hand and Toni took Maria's. Victoria looked up and smiled.

«It's curious,» Leandro said, «but it seems to me we never have been as happy as Victoria can be.»

* * *

Genaro took her hand and pulled her toward him.

«You see, my dear?»

«Thanks to the good Lord and to you.»

The sun shone as if ordered by the Mayor and by God.

Genaro said, «Yes, indeed, you will be up on top of the float and you will arrive at just the right moment; the stadium will go wild. The governor, the queen will already be there. . . everyone! It will be your triumphal entry. Sun and flowers and you above all!»

«You are a poet!» Zenaida said rubbing up against him.

«Silly. . .» he caressed her. «I will have the police band play a fanfare for your entrance. . . I will order everyone to give you a tremendous welcome.»

«Ah!» Zenaida said nibbling his collar. «You are my Genaro, the Genius.»

«You mean Genaro, the Genital. . .»

«What? . . Don't be coarse.»

«Come on, come on. . . it's our private language.»

* * *

Daniel propped his elbows on the table — a linen cloth embroidered by hand — and lit a cigarette. He thought of how serious he looked. He thought of how serious he ought to be. And, besides, he really was serious.

His mother continued, «. . . without the least regard for yourself. Do you understand? . . The servant knows, she sees you come and go away, and she sees you come back with lipstick on your shirt. . . It's very bad taste. . . What is she going to think?»

«She won't think much,» Daniel said and drank some more coffee. «In case she does, she'll be thinking about when it's her turn. . . She'll be more agreeable with me and put up with you longer. . . That's no problem!. . The problem is the way you're carrying on.»

«You're acting just like your father!»

«And you're doing to me the same thing you did to my father!»

«What?»

«You're running my life. . . But I'm not going to let you.»

«Daniel! Daniel! You. . .!»

«Oh, Mamá, nothing's going to happen to you and you're not going to get sick either. . . I can be very nice to you if you'll leave me alone. I love you, don't you realize that?»

«That's what I get for giving you a car! That's what I get for thinking you were like me!»

«Mamá . . .» Daniel very slowly took another sip of coffee. «I love you and I understand you. I am twenty-three years old. And remember! This is the first time I've ever spent the night out. Leave me alone!»

Lucía shot him a withering glance.

«You're just like your father!»

«And you're just like yourself!»

«Daniel!»

She didn't move. Daniel got up quickly and ran over to her: he hugged her.

«Forgive me, Mamá.»

Lucía, after a few minutes of immobility that seemed endless to him, stroked his cheek. In a hoarse voice she began, «It's odd. . . I didn't want to be stupid. . . Daniel. . . you are right. . . I. . . Son. . . I. . . I am getting old, you know? . . . Wait. . . my little Daniel. Daniel, I am not a fool. Thank you,» she caressed him. «Thank you. We have to talk about these things. . . without going to extremes. . . You know, I wanted you to be a girl, but you were a boy. Then, when you were growing up, I convinced myself that our differences wouldn't be any obstacle to our understanding each other — on the contrary. I. . . I know what you did last night. . . It hurts me — don't say anything — that you announce it with a dirty shirt. . . I am dirty, Daniel, I am . . . No, let me continue — I would have preferred you to sleep the first time with one of those girls in the town who wouldn't demand anything from you. . . And then

54

I was afraid and I asked myself, 'But if he doesn't know anything, how can he do it?' I know I love you and I hurt you. . . I thought that. . . as the years passed. . . you were so good. . . I thought. . . When you were very small, I told myself that I couldn't protect you from everything, but I didn't think that included me. . . Daniel. . . if you want me to, I can be content with him.» Daniel kissed her hands and hugged her.

«Mamá,» he begged, «Don't make me think now.»

«Daniel. . .» she murmured, «my son, I am an egotist. I am so selfish I want you to save me . . . my little Daniel.»

«Don't call me little Daniel,» he interrupted.

* * *

With the recording of *My Fair Lady* at full volume, Jacobo and Carmela were dancing:

> With a little bit of luck
> With a little bit of luck

Alicia, still in her robe, came running in and separated them abruptly.

«Margarita didn't sleep at home either!»

«What?»

«Really?»

The «either» made them think:

«Where?» (Carmela)

With Luis, he made it! (Jacobo)

Alicia had already thought: With Daniel.

«What do you think?» Alicia asked.

«Well,» Carmela began, «she probably stayed with a friend.»

«Yes! That's what I said, probably Alma Rincón. . . Her landlady, Doña Pacha, called me.»

Carmela interrupted, «That old gossip!»

Alicia went on, «And I told her I think she told us last night she was going to stay at Alma's house.»

«Yes, I'm sure she spent the night with Alma!»

«A pair of liars!» Jacobo cried. «You both think she spent the night with Daniel.»

«It doesn't matter to me,» — Alicia.

«Not to me either, she can sleep with anybody she wants to sleep with,» — Carmela (as long as it's not Hernán).

«Shall I tell you who?» Jacobo asked.

Their eyes widened.

«Do you know?»

«No, I'm guessing. . . She and Luis.»

«Yes,» — doubtfully.

«Yes, of course!»

«Yes, no doubt about it!»

«Yes, yes!» — both.

«Who told you?»

«No one told me anything, I'm just guessing. And I said it just to keep Alicia from bursting into tears, because I can't stand weepy women! . . Your precious Daniel spent last night with a broad, but don't worry, because what he learned, if you marry him some day, will be to your advantage. . .»

«What a dirty mind!»

«Filthy!»

Jacobo sang:

With a little bit of luck.

* * *

The slow progress of the truck finally came to a halt beside the statues at the stadium. The ride had been sad and Zenaida's cheeks were burning with embarrassment. She got up on the float in front of the new post office with some cheers of «Bravo Zenaida» «hurrah for Zenaida» from her cousins and aunts and uncles, and afterwards — nothing. The immense float went slowly down the entire length of Diego Leño without any applause, without anyone to admire her. When they got to Los Berros, she straightened up, pulled in her stomach, put her hands on her hips and was really beautiful — more than she imagined. But Los Berros was also empty; that is, the whole damp, mossy park was dotted with children of six to ten years old and their nursemaids. They saw her pass and admired her. Their eyes shone with appreciation and maybe they would never forget her. But Zenaida wasn't living for eternity or for minors. In a straight line they advanced along Díaz Mirón toward the stadium. She heard the music and a confused chorus of applause, cheers, clapping and yells. A drunk workman yelled, «What a classy piece of tail!»

And that was her only compliment. The obscenity annoyed her but later — a few seconds later — she thought that she should have smiled. After all he's an admirer and it's Carnival. . .

The boat, cone, pyramid, whatever it was, stopped at the foot of the statues. Zenaida distractedly looked at its base: azaleas, gardenias, chrysanthemums, orange blossoms, and at the top, the most beautiful flower of all, Zenaida López. She looked at herself, her body outlined in sequined mesh. . .

An indefinite sun. Clouds. . .

The rock-and-roll number finished, and when the applause died down, the announcer cried,

«And now, our comedians, Nick and Prick!»

Thunderous applause.

«I'm Nick.»

«No, he's Prick.»

«You're Prick.»

«You're the old Nick.»

«I'm a real Prick.»

The laughter kept her from hearing clearly. Zenaida was afraid — suppose Genaro doesn't come through? And lets me stay here waiting like a fool. She was just about to get down off the float, but a man came running up and said, «After them you go in. . . Everything is ready! . . When the applause stops. . . there'll be a silence. . . and then they'll play a fanfare. . . and you'll enter. . . as a queen! Better than queen!»

Zenaida lavished her best smile on him. Her cold sweat stopped. She took out her compact and looked at herself in the tiny mirror.

A flute-thin voice (Nick to Prick): «A friend came to Judas' house and knocked, Bam, bam, bam. The door opened and he asked, «Is Judas at home?» And they answered, «No, he's gone to a farewell dinner.»

Zenaida laughed, almost dropping her compact. «That's a good one. . .» she said to the man who was still looking at her.

You're the good one, he thought, smiling at her.

«Yes, it's a good one, all right.»

The comedians finished lamely and went off to light applause. Soon a trumpet sounded. . . a call to attention. . . Inexplicably (the surprise of the trumpet call, something not on the program) an absolute silence ran through the stands. . . And suddenly, before everyone appeared an enormous boat, cone, pyramid, with Zenaida at the top. A Zenaida never lovelier than at this moment. The closer she came the louder grew the applause and cries of admiration: an endless, unbounded enthusiasm,

«Beautiful! Beautiful!»

«Hurrah for Zenaida!»

«Bring her this way!»

«There is the queen!»

«Bravo, my Zena!»

«Bravo!»

«Hurrah for Zenaida!»

«Bravo!»

«Bravo!»

«Bravo!»

«Send her over here!»

«Send her over here!»

«Hurrah!»

«Go around again!»

«With each one!»

«Hurrah for Zenaida!»

«Hurrah!»

«Bravo, baby!»

«Bring her this way!»

«Hurrah for Zenaida, Hurrah for Zenaida, Hurrah for Zenaida!»

«Adios Zenaida!»

«How about a little dance?»

«Tum, tee, tum, tum. . .»

«Hurrah for the other queen!»

In front of the reviewing stand Zenaida's eyes shone for Genaro. She is so beautiful, Genaro thought.

«She's such an attractive girl,» — the wife of the governor.

And Zenaida said to herself, Lina, the First, is going to have a fit tonight. She had triumphed and now it could rain again.

* * *

«We have to go to Mass,» — Adriana.

«Don't be an idiot!» — Tino.

«It's Lent!»

«Look. . . You can divorce me! . . But let's fix up the house first, O.K.?»

* * *

«You. . .» Margarita begged.

«No,» Luis said firmly. «You first.»

Margarita jumped up. It wasn't cold, but she was trembling. Hesitating no longer, she ran toward the bathroom.

Luis, delighted, watched her disappear. A few seconds of silence and the noise of the shower. He threw back the sheet. Margarita pulled the curtain and turned to look at him. The water started falling on her shoulders; she closed her eyes, put her face under the spray and felt his arms, his body. With a curious sensation: like rubber, as if, under the water, skin had a different touch, consistency. The kiss was rubbery, too. Like a rubber doll.

«You have a beautiful body,» he said.

Luis was watching her, calculating, observing her, feeling himself possessor of something undeserved.

She, again timid, embraced him, felt him below, almost there. They kissed under the water. The sensation of rubber disappeared, her fingers ran over his body, touched him, discovered him. And he touched her also in a caress of recognition, a desire to feel her completely under this water. Sensing each other, bending their knees without separating their lips. Yes. The two of them. The one of them. The water wetting, in anticipation, their fulfilled desire. They. Two. One. A laughing kiss. . .

* * *

«In the dark forests of Calabria there lived a terrible band of thieves, sons of honorable men, even though they too were thieves. One day the chief of the band called Juan and said to him, «Juan, tell us a story,» and Juan began, «In the dark forests of Calabria there lived a terrible band of thieves, sons of honorable men, even though they too were thieves. One day the chief of the band called Juan and said to him, «Juan, tell us a story,» and Juan began,» «Stop!» Bartolomé cried.

«No, Pa, don't say that. Let me tell you the story,» and Ana started again.

* * *

Arnaldo said, «I hope I don't drink as much today as yesterday.»
«That's up to you.» Sara said.
«Me and my will power.» he declared.
«You'll drink. I know. You'll drink more today.» Leandro said.
«You should have invited Alma,» Sara said putting on her raincoat.
«Barbara would have been pleased.»
«Me, too. . . But. . . I'm still not sure.»
«She loves you,» Leandro said, opening the door.
«Oh, you conceited men!» Sara.

* * *

Clemen poured Borrito a glass of cognac, «Especially for you!» Then in a confidential tone, «Do you know what Zenaida López did today?»
The two of them snug in the enormous living room of Dr. Pereda. The walls covered by a tapestry new at the turn of the century, now torn and patched, almost colorless, the roses nearly gone along with the rigidly repeated, symmetrical Louis XV couples that had pleased Dr. Pereda so much. All dull, blurred, anachronistic and excessive; twelve ostentatious clocks (none of the twelve work); three guarded (each one) by a pair of masculine angels (all too obviously masculine). Five with Hércules at the side, all identical, as if mass produced. («It's disgraceful. . . they must have bought them by the dozen!») But they've never given anyone any. Another (everyone's favorite): a child in marble seated before a small stream holding a clock with gold numerals instead of a pitcher; she seems overwhelmed and pensive, it is the secret of her success. Placed at the main entrance, made of ebony, a pair of adolescents: in place of sex organs — their legs very wide open: they have clock faces with the numerals also of ebony and the hands of inlaid gold. It used to be — depend-

ing on the hour — the little hands seemed unpleasant and gross. The last clock: the eye of a Great Dane, something that tried to be funny. A one-eyed silver dog. The space left by the clocks is filled with small, marble-topped tables, crowded with all the dolls and animals that proudly decorate an average antique shop. Also there are fans, lockets, swords, flower bowls, immense vases, huge mirrors with hand worked frames, and from the ceiling two chandeliers hang. «I wouldn't sell them for less than fifty thousand. . . each. . .»

«What?» Borrito asked and straightened his trousers.

«You know who she is, don't you?» Clementina asked indicating that knowledge was fundamental to all she was going to add.

«Yes, of course,» Borrito answered in disgust, as if she had forgotten he was as much for Jalapa as she was and they knew the same people. «She's the granddaughter of Marcolfa Domínguez, the youngest daughter of Don Isidoro, the one that was a sweetheart, or whatever, of your uncle César and he almost married her, but it seems your papá didn't permit it, and I think my mother didn't either, because they say she had done something impolite. . . I don't know what. . . something that happened when Papá took her to the Casino the night of their first wedding anniversary. . . but. . . you know it all! . . Zenaida is the daughter of Pilar, the fat one, and Captain Eugenio López, the one that's been here. . . and no one used to have anything to do with him. . . ever since '37, isn't it? And I also know her. She's very attractive. . . even distinguished.»

«Well, yes.» Clemen interrupted. «Really fallen from grace.»

«What did she do?»

«Wait! . . Do you know whose girl friend she is?»

«No, who?»

«Well, you don't know anything yet!» Clemen sipped her cognac.

«Come on, I'm hungry!»

«Well, they say she's cozy with the mayor! . . With Genaro! . .» Clementina came to a complete stop and, arching her eyebrows, waited for a comment that didn't come. Irritated, she looked at him for several seconds and exploded, «Don't you know who Genaro is married to?»

«To my cousin Eugenia. . . so?»

«How cynical! You take everything so calmly! It's easy to see you live in Mexico City!»

«Well, poor old Genaro — married but not mutilated!»

«Coarse, vulgar!»

Clementina stood up and drank her cognac. «I don't know how I put up with you!»

«Come on. . . . come on.» Borrito interrupted. «Don't get carried away, we're two of a kind!»

«Two of a kind! What a comparison!»

«Listen, my family has more background than yours!»

«Yes, and more perversion, too; the Garzas are strong on that! Fairy!»

«You, too, . . I'm sure that. . . At least you wish you could!»

Clemen started to cry. Borrito stood up and embraced her.

«What a pair we are!» in a loving, conciliatory tone.

«Not me. Heavens! How you do go on!» but she let him hug her and leaned against him.

«To your health. . .» he said.

«To your health.»

They touched their glasses and smiled at each other.

«That Zenaida. . .» the indefatigable Clemen continued, «disgraced Eugenia today. She threw Genaro a kiss when she passed in front of the reviewing stand! Do you realize that?»

«Stop gossiping! Look, you haven't backed out, have you?»

«No!»

«Then, it's all set?»

«All set.»

* * *

Luis Rentería opened the door.

«Come in.»

He didn't hesitate. He seemed to expect it. However, there were a few embarrassed moments — a brief silence. A circumstance foreseen but not confirmed and now confirmed by confusion. Each one uncomfortable and consciously awkward sat in his usual place. Luis Rentería's narrow living room seemed even narrower. A cardboard moment — mute and absurd, like oversized toys. . .

Luis called:

«Margarita. . . they're here.»

* * *

Doña Pilar took her hand, came closer and kissed her cheek lightly. «You were magnificent,» she murmured leading her toward the living room. Doña Pilar was resplendent, wearing more jewelry than the queen herself — a sapphire bracelet and ring, emerald ear rings, a pearl necklace and a monumental ruby pin. «Today,» she said earlier, while she was dressing, «we're going to go all out.» Her aqua blue dress of Italian silk, draped over her bosom and at her waist, did nothing to diminish her two hundred and six pounds, but it pleased her greatly. Her breasts, hips, and the folds of cloth bounced happily as she bore Zenaida along. «Magnificent, magnificent. . .» she repeated with little chirps. For Doña Pilar Beteta de López this Carnival Sunday was a long awaited revenge and her face could only reflect the satisfaction of success — a happiness that was compensation for all the humiliations she had endured from the people of Jalapa; humiliations still remembered and written down in a Diary of Insults begun in 1935, when the captain had come to Jalapa. Today, almost twenty-four years later, this long-awaited Sunday arrived reconciling and triumphant.

She stopped in the entrance to the living room, squeezed the arm of her daughter to keep her from going in first, and when she saw everyone was looking at them, took a step forward and exclaimed.

«Zenaida, the First. . . and the Queen Mother!»

Zenaida pulled away brusquely from her grip and cried, «Mamá, don't say such foolish things!»

Doña Pilar's answer couldn't be heard because of the applause. Zenaida walked quickly toward her father. The Captain put his glass down and embraced his daughter. Zenaida kissed his hard skin, full of grey stubble, breathed in the strong tobacco and sweat smell of her father and was surprised to see, over his shoulder, the face of Doña Hermila Ferrón. Really, she thought, today is a day of triumph for my mother. . . not for me.

Doña Hermila held out both arms to her.

«My dear!» she pressed two kisses on each cheek.

«May I kiss you, too?» Don Pedro, red with cognac and pleasure, asked in a loud voice.

Zenaida shrugged her shoulders and with an enchanting smile exclaimed.

«If you still can!»

Don Pedro Ferrón also gave her four very loud kisses, thinking, «If you only knew.»

At one end of the room, Doña Asunción nudged Doña Belén and whispered,

«The girl has flair.»

«And distinction,» Doña Belén answered. «No one can take that away from her.»

«The years will take it away. You'll see!» Doña Toña put in, thinking of herself. She sighed.

The three ladies stood up to kiss Zenaida.

And the three to themselves, She's very daring.

«Zenaida,» Doña Pilar explained, «is angry because I called her the queen, but wouldn't you say she's prettier than Lina?»

«Mamá. . .»

Doña Pilar continued, «This little girls is so shy. . . I, at her age!»

«A toast!» Captain López called.

Doña Hermila went to Zenaida and took her aside.

«Here I am, during Lent, only to see you. God will forgive me because of you, child, you're as lovely as the Virgin!»

Doña Pilar had joined them.

«Yes. . . poor Doña Hermila, we are very gratified, it's a sacrifice for her. . . to go out to such things during Lent.»

«Yes, . . well, no. I am sinning because I am lying. I was glad to come. . . But my priest, I mean my son, won't like it.»

«Is he your confessor?» Doña Pilar asked in astonishment.

«Oh, no, what a sacrilege! To a mother a son is always a son.»

«Of course! This one is still my daughter even though she is the queen.»

«Mamá! . . Let's drink a toast! . . Excuse me, Carlín is calling me. . .»

Carlín, myopic, chubby and repugnant (a friend since childhood) put his arm around her shoulders. «Let's drink one, you and me for . . . you know who!»

«Do I?» she responded, looking at her watch. Genaro probably was having dinner at Bartolomé Soto's. «Cheers! . . Excuse me, I'm going to take off these tights.»

«They fit you like a glove,» Carlín said.

«They're made to order, idiot!»

*   *   *

«Alma Rincón doesn't have a phone and she lives by herself, so if you want to, we could say you spent the night with her,» Alicia said.

«Let's go see her now and get it fixed up.» — Carmela.

Margarita smiled.

«No, thanks. Luis and I have agreed. We're not hiding anything. From now on we're going to live together.»

«Without planning to get married?» Alicia asked.

«Yes. . . yes, we are planning to.»

«What a woman!» Carmela exclaimed jokingly. «If I had your nerve, I'd sleep with Hernán tonight.»

«And I'd sleep with Bartolomé,» Alicia said.

«No, no,» Carmela cried. «You can't get mixed up with the married ones. You have to start with a bachelor. And anyway, Barbara is very attractive, don't you think? . . And the married ones are easy but tricky. First I'll throw myself at Hernán, or some one else if he doesn't come across and then, with my experience. . .» she turned to Margarita, «O.K., tell us; I've only read about it.»

Margarita and Alicia burst into laughter.

All three were laughing when the men came back from the store with bottles of rum, vermouth, and red wine; bread, canned meats and cheese.

«Ready,» Luis said.

«Let's have a drink,» — Jacobo.

«Páez, the sponge, you'll never stop drinking. No wonder you're such a blimp,» Alicia said rumpling his hair. «Did you make the calls?»

«In the first place,» Jacobo said threatening her with the bottle of wine, «don't you dare call me a blimp, you have a couple of plump spots yourself a little lower than your shoulders, and, in the second place. . .»

«You're awful!»

«I did call your Daniel, but there seems to be a mix-up at his house . . . I didn't understand very well.»

«And when *do* you understand very well?»

«It seems his folks are going to patch things up and he has to wait until his father calls long distance. . . or I don't know what and it doesn't matter. He says he can come around five o'clock.»

«And Hernán?»

«Your Hernán was sleeping off a hangover with his conscience aching, too! He'll be here in twenty minutes to get cured.»

«Jacobo is an angel!»

«Without equal,» he finished.

«We're going to call Batuta for you,» Luis said. «He lives near here.»

«Well, he's better than nothing,» Carmela shrugged her shoulders. «I just hope he won't be a nuisance.»

«First I need to know if Batuta will accept me. Maybe I'm not his type.»

«Well. . . all right, all right,» Margarita cried. «A toast to the happy couple!»

«Yes. . . to the newly-weds!»

«Look, look,» Carmela cried. «She's blushing!»

Margarita reddened and seemed on the verge of tears. Luis ran to embrace her and gave her a kiss.

Then, as if it were a real wedding, Carmela and Alicia came up to kiss her and Jacobo gave Luis an *abrazo*.

«To the happy couple!»

A toast, may we make it three couples tomorrow!»

«And what about me?» — Jacobo.

«Luis, please call Batuta.»

* * *

«Papá, may I play?»

«Yes, go ahead and play.»

Toni sat down on the rug at their feet and dialed a number on his toy telephone.

«Hello?» . . Santa Claus?»

Adriana asked, «Is it Santa Claus who brings you toys?»

«No, of course not! . .» Bartolomé said. «It's the Three Wise Men.»

«The Three Wise Men,» Ana repeated watching them.

«And so?» Tino asked picking Toni up and putting him on his knee. «Why are you talking to Santa Claus?»

«Because Papá buys the things Santa Claus brings,» Ana said.

Everyone laughed. Toni observed them.

«Yes, what Ana said is true, isn't it, Ana?»

«Barbara,» Bartolomé begged, «have María come take them.»

«But, my darling,» Barbara said ingenuously, «we're not doing anything bad.»

Even more laughter.

«Children. . . children,» Barbara called. «María is going to give you some cookies.»

The two children ran out toward the kitchen.

«As I see it,» Genaro Almanza said, «now comes the good part, right?»

Laughter again while Barbara and Sara refilled the glasses.

«Genaro just loves to joke!» Eugenia said arching her eyebrows. «Our children are going to be revised editions of ourselves.»

«Our children will be degenerates!» Arnaldo Wells pronounced.

«Arnaldo, please,» Bartolomé begged, «we aren't going to have them cooperatively.»

«Talk about your own,» Sara finished.

The telephone rang and a few moments later María came in to say, «For Señor Almanza.»

Genaro put down his glass, made a slight bow to excuse himself, and, avoiding his wife's eyes, went rapidly toward the hall.

«Genaro Almanza. . .»

«It's me. I have to talk to you.»

«Why?»

«I'm happy. . . Thank you for everything! My entrance was like a dream.»

«Un huh.»

«Can't you talk?»

«You know Eugenia is here.»

«But I also have some rights. . . and anyway, I take all the risk. She doesn't take any.»

«Of course not. She's my wife and that's a different matter.»

«Oh, you're in a bad mood!»

«No, you put me in one.»
«Well, see you later!»
«Tonight.»
«What do you think?»
«You know.»
«No.»
«Definitely.»
He went back to sit next to his wife. The laughter continued.
Tino Remes was telling about something that happened in Paris. In a low
voice, Eugenia asked Genaro, «Business?»
«Dinner is ready!» Barbara announced. «Time for dinner!»

* * *

Alma Rincón observed the enormous corridor — on Sunday the silence
always made it seem larger. . . (in four more hours she would see him). As
rigid as if — by willing it — she could convert herself into a statue, into absolute inerita: into death. As if (by not moving again, ever again) everything
that turns oscillates walks jumps creeps flies could be paralyzed. As if. . .
She started to walk down the long corridor. She turned rapidly and went
toward the room leaving behind her the endless row of flower pots —
geraniums, wisteria, primroses, ferns, jasmine, orchids, violets, lilies — the
only witnesses to the immensity and silence of the corridor. Her high heels
struck the mosaic noisily — in an ever increasing rhythm until it died away on
the carpet of the living room and there she began to cry for no reason at all, as
if she could, through her tears, become a child again, or as if, more exactly,
tears could bring her close to him, to Arnaldo. Because he would understand,
he did understand her, because. . .
She stood up, smiled. . . saw herself in the mirror. . . I look like a
hysterical old maid. . . No. No, I'm not. No, I'm not.
Her green cotton dress made her eyes seem a lighter green. Very tall, in
the mirror — because of its slant — her head almost touched the chandelier.
An odd effect. There she looked beautiful, fascinating, how does Arnaldo see
me? How? . . . She smiled as she was used to smiling at him, but nothing seemed real. There was an Alma Rincón — herself — that she would never know. .
her movements, the way she acted in front of others, not to a mirror, her
laugh, her voice, above all her voice. . . its tone, the sound of her laughter. . . I
will never know.
She ran to her bedroom, grabbed her purse, checked the contents: thirty-
two pesos. Plenty. Two handerkerchiefs, perfume, keys, lipstick, powder,
mirror . . . I'll get a cab at the corner . . . No, first I'll call Alicia . . . They're
probably there or at Luis' house.

Oh sad is the day and sad the . . . words I say because you took
the bus and . . . went away Oh sad is the day . . . it's desola-a-a-
tion chón — chón — chón — chón

Hernán looked astonished for a few seconds, or still asleep. Luis held the
door open and said, «Come in.»

Alicia and Carmela were singing and dancing together.

«What's with those two? . .» Hernán asked. «On the stuff?»
They danced and sang even louder.

Oh sad is the day and sad the . . . words I say because you went
away . . .
chón — chón — chón — chón

«Come on, come on! Quiet down!» Jacobo cried. «You're going to scare
little Hernán who just woke up . . . Here, little boy, here's your ration of
rum.»

Perspiring, the girls stopped dancing and came over. Carmela kissed
Hernán on the cheek and yelled, «It's Carnival . . . Carnival! Down with
sobriety.»

«Me, too!» Alicia said, and kissed Hernán also.

«How about me?» Jacobo asked. «Not man enough?»

Both of them hugged and kissed him.

«Now a toast to the newly-weds,» Luis proposed.

«Who?» Hernán asked.

«Us . . .» Luis embraced Margarita and kissed her on the lips.

«What a bunch of drunks! Last night got to everybody but me!»

«It's true!»

«Oh!»

«Yes . . . They're married!»

«Husband and wife.»

«Hurrah for the newlyweds!»

Margarita went over to Hernán, took his hand and, smiling, said, «Really . . . we got married.»

«And we're going to get married, too,» Luis said hugging her again.

Hernán understood at last. His first smile was transformed and there appeared on his face something indescribably childish that made him defenseless
and ingenuous.

«To the newlyweds!»

«Come on,» Clementina said taking him by the hand.

They were enveloped in shadow and the scent of moth balls and quince. Something that made both of them remember childhood — those rarely opened closets, full of secrets and treasures . . . Clemen let go of his hand and drew the curtains. In the grey light, the room briefly took on the appearance of a desecrated tomb.

«Let's look for . . .»

* * *

When she realized no one could see her, she stopped smiling. The big black Packard rolled over the wet pavement. Don Pedro very slowly turned toward the left and descended by the side of the new Post Office. Everything seemed to glisten. She took several deep breaths of the clean, damp air as if trying to purify herself.

«You and your foolishness!» she exploded finally.

Don Pedro had expected it before. Calmly he started driving around Los Berros. Without irony he answered,

«Remember it's Lent.»

«A fine time for you to remember! . . Completely shameless! . . . As if you had to remind me of it! . . As if you didn't make me go! . .»

«Make you, no,» he responded. He was driving very serenely. His face was flushed, almost purple, but he seemed very calm.

«I have endured so many things,» she protested.

«*We* have, Hermila, *we* have . . .»

«But you made me!» she complained as they started up the stadium hill. «You made me!»

She said it threateningly and Don Pedro knew very well she really wanted to say, I will tell Efrén you made me. But to Don Pedro those things were not important. He could drive peacefully avoiding the chuckholes, not answering, almost not hearing.

«First there is obligation,» he murmured, «and then devotion . . . Captain López will be my associate, we have to get along well with him . . . He invited us . . . I couldn't refuse him . . . You, as a good wife, had to be at my side . . . As always . . . It is your duty . . . Isn't it? . . . That's what you tell me every day . . . What we have to do» — his voice monotonous while the car moved along more and more slowly — «our daily bread . . . And anyway you introduced me to Doña Pilar and the Captain . . . She's also very religious, isn't she?»

«That's a different matter . . . The thing that bothers me is the girl. . .»

* * *

«. . . now Mamá is going to talk to you. . .» Daniel handed her the phone. Lucía trembled.

«Yes. . . I. . .»

Daniel went out into the hall. He preferred leaving her alone; they could talk better that way. He entered his bedroom, put on his jacket and looked at himself in the mirror. He was pale. It was the first time in his life he had not slept all night, but he wasn't sleepy. He had to get out of the house. He thought of Alicia Carmela Margarita Alma Jacobo Hernán Luis Carnival. He dropped his car keys on the dresser. He didn't need them. Then he knotted his tie and went out.

Mamá was still on the phone. Daniel threw her a farewell kiss. She lifted her eyebrows slightly.

«Come back soon.»

He nodded, already in the doorway, where she could no longer see him. The air was cold; there was a light drizzle, the end of the street was lost in fog. Daniel smiled. As always, he told himself, I have gotten more involved than I should, more than they suppose. The «Come back soon» was for me, and Papá is going to think. . . But. . . Funny, maybe it was really for him and she didn't see me go out. . . It's possible. . . Everything is possible.

He walked faster. In spite of the cold and fog, the streets were full of people. Daniel moved against the crowd going away from the center of town. In the middle of the street some revellers dampened by tequila and rain *Zum zum zum zum zum ba, bae, zum zum zum zum zum ba, pájaro lindo de la madrugá, pájaro lindo de la. . .* Behind them a group of children imitating the rhythm, twistings and turnings and farther on, more merrymakers: amusing cats in black flannel, with young girls inside, one called, «Bet you don't know me, Daniel Orozco, bet you don't know me.»

Daniel smiled. A cat threw him kisses. And suddenly they surrounded him, shrieking, mewing, holding hands to make a circle, sing-songing:

Marisola h-e-e-e-re
Marisola th-e-e-e-re
all day
all night
keeping us aw-a-a-a-ke.

Daniel tried to recognize them but couldn't.

«Now you have to kiss everyone,» one of them proposed as their song ended.

«Better for us to kiss him or he'll just be kissing cloth.»

They all jumped on him and kissed him. Suddenly a red-haired witch appeared.

«Beasts/ Beasts! Opportunists! I'm going to get Alicia Esteva!»

With a small wand she began hitting them. Strident, exaggerated cries of pain filled the street and then the witch shrieked when she was attacked by all the cats. She started running and shouting, closely pursued by the others. Daniel smiled and quickly climbed the steps to Luis Rentería's apartment. He pounded on the door.

Hernán opened it.

«What forfeit does he pay?» Carmela asked.

«Let him tell what happened last night,» Alicia said with mock seriousness.

«Good for Alicia!»

«Tell us!»

«All right,» Daniel agreed, «but it's a pornographic tale. . . Once upon a time, long, long ago. . .»

«First: a toast to the newlyweds!»

Daniel got in on the secret. too: like Hernán, like Alma (she had arrived an hour before) he thought at first they were kidding him.

* * *

«Bet you don't know who I am!»

«Bet you don't know who I am!»

* * *

Cries, shrill, falsetto, halfway to happiness halfway fun. Carnival. Alma tucked her legs, huddled into the couch and for a few seconds — that seemed eternal — looked at the geometric design of the upholstery: Small green stains crossed by black lines converted into brown angles, united on an orange point and, again small green stains . . . Grey background. Grey stained by ashes, liquor, red wine, dust. Cries came up from the street; rising three floors, coming in through the windows. That brief happiness of Jalapa came through: It's Carnival! . . It's a miracle, it's a who knows what but you have to agree, you feel it, I feel it and there is, in spite of the absence of everything, I know that within me exists an echo, something that approves and gives consent and yes it is Carnival today, now, right now is Carnival, I see this coarse weaving, not coarse, this green, orange, black, grey at times merges like the rhythm of the record Carmela played and all of them, I too, filling ourselves with something to go down and down, and arrive there in the center of the city, and suddenly, no not suddenly, because we knew for months before, we come back happy and what difference does it make about Arnaldo, what difference, really, that I, in front of me, the window where I see a little bit of tiny Jalapa and I hear the record Carmela put on and the cries from over there, and where are you, you are where, why don't you come, you said you would come, here, that in any case we would see each other at the Emir, but no, here first, if you wanted to see me, to be just the two of us, we would go together, Arnaldo you know I've already had three glasses of wine today and two of anis or maybe four, and now I'm drinking who knows what?

She took a sip. Rum. The room danced a noiseless waltz. Waltz. Waltz. .

* * *

The wall of the castle began at the edge of the last red mosaic, a few steps farther, without a clear limit, the cliff, and below, many feet below, the sea crashed on the rocks making a strange menacing sound, almost words, almost voices revealing an important secret. Like the noise of sea shells held to the ear, only multiplied a thousand times. They were protected by the solid wall of chairs. Sitting and lying comfortably on rugs of newspapers, sipping coffee from empty cups. Their heads adorned with caps of crepe paper decorated with silver dust. On the rugs the remains of a confetti orgy. . . The princess suddenly seized the hands of the queen and begged,

«Victoria, come to live with us. Tell Mamá you want to be my nanny.»

«But I work for Señora Sara, Ani, I can't.»

«María could go with her and you could stay with us.»

«So you don't love me?» María asked, pretending a great sadness, that in reality she did feel to some extent.

«Yes, María, I do love you, but I love Victoria more.»

«I love you more, María,» Toni said, hugging her. «I'm going to give you my confetti rolls so you can throw them tonight in the park.»

«Thank you, sweetie,» she kissed him. «But I'm not going to the park tonight. Your Mamá and Papá are going out and I'm going to stay to take care of you.»

Ana got up.

«Victoria, come go with me,» she ordered.

Together they ran across the rugs, leaving the castle and entering the dark studio. There was light in the living room and the sound of her father's and Uncle Leandro's voices. She took Victoria's hand and they went up the steps.

In front of the dressing table Sara and Barbara were putting on make-up.

«Mamá, may Victoria spend the night with us? . .»

«Ask your Aunt Sara.»

«Can she? Is it all right?»

«If Victoria wants to, she may stay.»

Victoria thought of the fireworks she was not going to see.

«Yes, señora.»

* * *

«You're my partner, whether you like it or not,» Jacobo said, pulling her up. «Now we all have partners.»

«To each his own,» Alicia said dancing cheek to cheek with Daniel.

«For the moment,» Alma answered, placing her cheek against Jacobo's. The physical contact with him was like a cold shower, something that restored her serenity, a kind of half serenity immediately attacked and invaded by memories — that skin, Jacobo's, could be, is, if I want, Arnaldo's skin. . .

But no. Suddenly sober, she was dancing to perfection, with that admirable perfection that told her how to move her feet, to follow her partner, to move forward, to move back, she was dancing. Everybody was back in his place, inside Luis' tiny apartment (Luis' and Margarita's from today on):

«Beautiful! Beautiful!»

«Who?» Margarita asked.

«Me? Are you referring to me?» Carmela fluttered her eyelashes several times.

«No,» Alma cried. «Me. . .»

«Such a modest girl!» Alicia exclaimed.

«I mean,» Alma declared, «I have a beautiful hangover. Hurrah for the University's existentialists!»

«Forward! Forward! Proud colleagues!»

«Bravo for Arts and Science!»

«Bravo for Law!»

«Bravo again!»

«Again!»

Hernán burst out laughing and said, «If Professor Montes could see us, the University would be closed and the brilliant students kicked out.»

«Jewels!» Carmela corrected him. «Everyone here is a jewel!»

«Diamonds in the rough!» Jacobo.

«In the rough, in the rough, in the rough, but diamonds. . . Don't you think I'm in the rough — tell me, you guys, don't you think I'm unpolished?»

And everyone thought yes, because if Carmela wanted to, she could be the most attractive one of all. There she was in front of them suddenly rigid, her hands in her belt, head thrown back, teeth sparkling, hair still swinging with the music, her bosom rising and falling, rising temptingly, virgin beautiful.

*　*　*

Arnaldo observed his bare feet. He wiggled his toes. He rested.

His small bachelor apartment, the entire right wall covered with books, the bookcase — of soap boxes — almost touched the ceiling. A grey ceiling, stained, its monotony geometrically broken at the center where an extra long cord hung with a light bulb at the end. Unable to create any feeling. Except the heat of the bulb. The left wall — the one toward the street — with a window in the center. A window open now. Filtering through it all the scandalous noises of downtown: music cries insults screeching brakes music. Masquerades: maracas and cowbells, marimbas, guitars. . . After all and above all: himself. . . Himself reduced to the limits of his own body. Almost not existing. He alone. I. Here. . . At times he felt his legs, arms, chest, belly . . . If he wanted. But he had to will it, had to think: I will move my arm now because I want to get a cigarette. . . And so, as if in the final analysis the physical were invention and only *knowing* the physical could give existence to the physical. . . But there is salvation. One knows he has to move even though he doesn't want to because the body has needs: thirst, hunger, to urinate, something. . . And I have to get up and then all these stupidities that I regret and I tell myself they don't matter because it is Carnival and Alma is waiting for me. . . Alma. . . Soul. . . Why did they give you that name? It seems as if to me, a sceptic, but am I a sceptic? I'm not anything! Not even a sceptic! No, I can't! This is the way I am. It is not that I am betraying anyone. Moreover I wouldn't let myself betray anyone it's just that at times one looks at his legs and it seems that he sees something different and for the first time it would be within his grasp to comprehend what is reality what is missing in all our knowledge and in our own image, because it can't be accepted that I am this foot that moves itself because a shoe, a bit of new leather — relatively new — has pinched it; or it is oppression that can bring us close to our essence. Shoes and classes. Also classes of shoes. . . And I have to get up, but it will only be for her. I wouldn't have much to do outside. Or would I? . . Alma, I will never be worthy of you. . . Never. I know that. . . No, no I don't know anything. It's our destiny and if anyone invented the word I don't have to take the blame, do you think so, Alma, do you? I tell you I really want to move and that I would like Carnival to be over so everything would be the way it was before. Even though we might be more serious and dull. Even though we might not dare. . . You know, Alma, you know because you love me. . . And that is not the important thing. In spite of the fact that your face follows me — your face etched with love, definitely in spite of that. Yes. I was the one who chose you. And I will love you. . . Very much. . . Look at me here alone. . . You will have to. . . Not here. . . . Somewhere else. . . We'll look for a place: something that will be ours. I try to keep you out and you won't stay out and here you are superimposed on my egotism. You. Alma. I love you. Give me strength to get up. Tell me you are waiting for me anxiously and it doesn't matter — No! that *yes,* it does matter to you that I haven't come — Tell me, yes . . . yes? . . I, this skinny pig called Arnaldo, I, Alma, I love you. . .

*   *   *

A half hour after they were seated, the waiter finally brought the «meent-juleeps.» They had ordered them a little bit because they were feeling young (although when they were young, they never had dared order them) because they were the stylish drink in those days. No one wanted to go home and they thought as long as it was a holiday they might as well make the most of it. Also Captain López's sherry had considerably influenced their decision. Now the three «women of the world,» as Doña Asunción thought when they sat down at the table, were not inclined to go to bed at nine o'clock.

«I don't know why I ordered this mint-flavored junk.»

«Really,» Doña Asunción declared, «I don't either, I never liked the flavor. My grandmother used to insist on putting mint leaves on her temples when she had a headache and she said it was marvelous.»

«I remember,» — Doña Belén — «when I was a girl, my cousins and I ate it with a little salt on each leaf.»

«Well,» — Doña Toña — «I never could get it down.»

«What a fool you are, you were the one who ordered it for all of us!»

«If I weren't a fool, I wouldn't be a widow.»

«You mean you could have saved Ramon's life?» Doña Belén asked, astonished.

«Don't be an idiot! I mean if I weren't a fool, I would have gotten married again!»

«Now, now,» Asunción interrupted. «You're with friends who have known you forever. Don't brag to us!»

«I'm not lying!»

«Well» — Doña Belén, — «you were just as beautiful as ever. . . At the funeral you looked lovely.»

«But without a cent! Remember! Both of you remember! How well I know the story. . .»

«Well, if we came to fight. . .»

«No, not to fight: we're ladies. But if it comes to airing dirty linen. . .» and Antonia challenged them.

«How touchy!» Asunción protested. «It must be the menopause.»

«You were the first one to have the menopause,» Antonia declared. «Remember I gave you the first shots.»

«Asún, Toña! Please! Even the boys at the next table are listening to you! Don't you have any shame?»

Asunción and Antonia looked at the boys together.

Zenaida appeared in the entrance at that moment.

* * *

«Those old witches!» Zenaida exclaimed furiously. «They're all over the

place! You find them all over Jalapa! At their age they should stay home!»
Genaro guided the automobile down hill quite satisfied with the meeting.
«Don't be so hard on them. After all, they have a right to enjoy
themselves one day a year.»
«To enjoy themselvs, yes. . . If it's possible to enjoy yourself at their age!
But not to gossip! Definitely not! . . Did you see them? Imagine what they are
saying about me!»
«And what you are saying about them!»
«But I am young!»
«They were, too. . . one time.» Genaro answered laughing.
«Oh, don't be so boring! . . If I had thought about what I will be when I
am old, I assure you I would not be here with you. So you'd better not talk
about futures and ages.»
«Well, I. . .»
«Turn around and go back. Don't think you are going to sleep with me
tonight. . . Only a husband has the right to demand that. . . A husband or a
wife. . . and you, my love, can demand it of Eugenia, your dear, dull
Eugenia!»
«Look,» Genaro made a U turn and went back toward town, «I'm not
going to rape you, we'll go back.»
«That's better!»
«Much better!» he answered suddenly aggressive. «I'll leave you in the
Arcade and you can stay there and do whatever you feel like doing. Your
'Queen Mother' is crazier than you and she approves of it all.»
Zenaida slapped him.
The car suddenly started zigzagging.

* * *

«To dance the *bamba*!» Leandro repeated, lighting his cigarette with
great difficulty. «To dance the *bamba* you need. . !»
«To dance on the table! To dance on the table! To dance on the table!»
Bartolomé cried.
Barbara went over to him and gave him a pinch.
«You are cruel!» she murmured. «I don't like you this way!»
Bartolomé turned toward her.
«This way? I don't like you this way either!»
Sara halfway heard them.
«This is no day for quarreling. . . Look at my husband!»
Leandro was laboriously climbing onto a chair and then the table. The
others quickly removed the glasses and he started to dance the *bamba*.

She's a cutie in a dance hall
She's a cutie in a dance hall
Her new shoes are hurting
But she's busy flirting. . .
And she goes up
And she goes up

and he goes down. He almost fell on top of them, on Bartolomé and Barbara. Bartolomé quickly stood up and tried to catch him but before he could get there, other hands reached Leandro: three pairs of hands: three masked faces. . .

«Bravo for Professor Montes!»

«Hurrah!»

Now Sara blushed and seemed about to cry as the masqueraders set Leandro on the floor.

«Have a drink!» Leandro cried. «I'm inviting you to have a drink. . . You saved my life!»

«You mean your reputation!» Bartolomé said.

«Yes,» Leandro said. «It would be ugly. . . Very ugly. . . Wouldn't it, Sara? . . A professor flat on the floor. . . I want you to have a drink.»

* * *

The drizzle falls slowly: a winter rain that one can trace almost from the clouds to the ground. Tonight is Carnival Sunday. Time to have fun. The rain and fog are part of the game. The rain adds to the pleasure: it makes the confetti stick to the faces of passersby, on their eyebrows, on their lips, on their noses, in their laughter. . . Laughing, one also swallows that final mossy drizzle of Winter. And faces laughter cries have another meaning and another charm under fog that can make irreality and mystery believable. Lucky people. They have here within reach of their hand, job, dream still another mystery. . . An unexpected mystery, close but never attainable. It is the fog — its play and effect on Carnival. Rumba dancers already unmasked and drunk. In their faces the overflowing flush of the last drink they can hold: a hiccough that slips out as a shout and whisper. The fog that turns the ugliest face into a promise. People run, splashing in the sea of confetti and unattainable dreams. Sometimes the fog disappears, returns them to themselves and when it seems gone, comes back again and starts the game all over. The children are closest to the heart of the mystery; they run tirelessly along the main street to the steps of the Cathedral where the crowd swallows them; there the people are joined all together; they dance; they dance who knows with whom or with what rhythm, but they dance, push, quarrel, shout, sing, dance and the fog makes them beautiful and ephemeral. No one can get into Juárez Park; there are so many people they can scarcely move. Occasionally flannel cats pass by. Witches with mop heads, masqueraders, two, two hundred, two thousand masqueraders who try to increase the mystery and laughter, the surprise, the fun. Every one dances to his own music, drinks from his own bottle, sings whatever he wants to sing. The women, all of them, let themselves be carried along by this impetus, shout when they are pushed and pinched, run away, scream with laughter, run away to join another group.

A thousand orchestras play. The rain doesn't matter. Everyone is already wet. So. What matters is laughing and they laugh. And throw confetti.

* * *

An old woman, dressed in black, appears and crosses the main street. She elbows her way along, pushing and being pushed. They shout insults at her throw confetti on her. She doesn't notice. She has come from the house of Falcón, the architect. She says a Rosary and makes a mistake on the Third Mystery. Then she repeats it confidently with no error and can't understand how she could have forgotten.

* * *

«Batuta!»

«Batuta, wait for us!»

But he runs away. He has seen them go into the arcade: they are going to the Emir. He is going to catch up with them. Someone yells behind him but he pays no attention, he wants to be with the gang, to be their friend, to tell them that he has a car they can use, and also a little house on the road to Veracruz where you can have as much fun as you like. Batuta runs. Some girls throw confetti on him. You have to be a good sport. Batuta runs. What's more you know lots of things about them. Last night you saw Margarita go into the building where Luis lives and you haven't told anyone. Absolutely no one. You are waiting to see them and tell them. . . that. . . that. . . But it's not time! . . No! It looked like. . .

Batuta stops breathless, leans against the wall. Soon he discovers Carlín.

«What are you doing hiding here?» he asks.

Carlín smiles.

«Watching,» he answers.

Two can-can dancers go by. They have stockings over their faces and they are screaming. Suddenly one falls to the ground. Her companion asks in a low voice,

«Did you hurt yourself?»

She gets up quickly, shows her legs to those who saw her fall, and in a falsetto voice exclaims,

«I feel like I'm eight months pregnant! Run, or I'll lose it right here!»
And they start running and dancing.

* * *

Here comes the sea serpent, sea serpent, sea serpent. . . They all went in — Carmela first and the others in a line behind.

A Mexican woman making lots of loot
selling plums and melons and other fruit
Little gold bell let me through
with all my kiddies but the one behind
Bim bam bim bam bam

They made their way through the tables around the edge of the Casino's lower dance floor.

Asunción swallowed the last of her «meent-juleep» and nudged Antonia.

«Look, there's Luis Esteva's daughter!»

«Nacha's girl?» Doña Toña asked, putting on her glasses.

«She's tight,» Belén said.

The line passed close by and Alicia and Carmela greeted them.

People started clapping, and the orchestra director up above, thinking it was time to begin the music, ordered a fanfare.

With the first chords the group doubled their enthusiasm following the rhythm of the fanfare with fast, grotesque movements. At the finale Carmela was in the center of the dance floor imitating a circus performer she had seen when she was eleven years old, throwing kisses at the crowd and bending her knees comically,

«Thank you! Thank you, kind people!»

Hernán, dying with laughter, took her arm and pulled her to the table where the rest were sitting down.

* * *

«I thought you would never come,» Alma said. She leaned against the wall and passed her tongue over her lips savoring his kiss.

«Me, too,» Arnaldo said kissing her again.

«Why?» she asked moving away from him. For a moment the light hit her eyes and made them fleetingly green.

«When someone has lived alone for a long time, he thinks he can imagine company.»

They were at the entrance of the Casino Jalapeño. Alma leaned against him, let herself be embraced briefly and said,

«We ought to go in with them. . .»

* * *

The orchestra conductor, whose taste was very Mexican, ordered: «The Jarabe Tapatío.»

«The young people stayed in their seats waiting for the next number. The street door opened at that moment and a pair of ballerinas made a triumphal entry, took possession of the dance floor and, in spite of the music, danced a can-can.

«They're good!» Alicia said.

«They dance well,» Toña commented.

«Who are they?» Asunción asked.

«They're darling,» Carmela exclaimed.

«A little indecent.»

«A little?»

«That one's bosom is fake.»

«How can you tell?»

«It's time for Higinio to be here.»

«Cuba libres for all of us.»

«No, coca cola.»

«Did you call him?»

«Hypocrite!»

«He knows very well this is where he can find me.»

«Look at those terrific faces!»

«You mean terrific cheek!»

«They're charming, they really are!»

* * *

Zenaide opened the car door.

«Free and equal, remember,» she said before getting out.

«No, wait,» he took her hand.

«Wait for what? . . To hide again? . . Or worse yet, so you can hide? No, big boy! We'll lose our reputation together. . . or you can keep your hots. . . if you have any hots left!»

«Imbecile!» he grabbed her and kissed her. «As if I were afraid! . . It's for your sake, only for you, understand? . . If only we had some hoods . . .»

Someone stuck his head through the door and smiled.

«Hello!» Carlín said.

«What do you want?» Zenaida said defiantly.

«Nothing! I saw you and came over. . . I heard something about hoods. . If you want, I can go buy some. . . the Nuevo Japón is still open.»

«How much do they cost?» Genaro asked.

«Twenty-five pesos each. . . Seventy-five pesos in all, one for me, too.»

Genaro gave him a hundred peso bill.

«Go around by the jail. . . find a parking place . . . I'll look for you there,» and Carlín started running.

*   *   *

Adriana pushed forward with difficulty, clutching Tino's hand. She was completely confused, it was cold and raining, but the people didn't mind; on the contrary, it seemed to increase their euphoria.

They went into the arcade. Tino told her, «Stay close beside me.»

Slowly they made their way through the crowd. A group of drunk mariachi players passed close by. Everyone was pushing everyone else. The heat was thick, hazy and deafening. The marimbas the mariachis the orchestra and the thousands of drunks who sang their own songs according to their memories or their tastes rather than the music. Adriana stopped shivering, feeling suffocated from lack of air. Tino moved along greeting all the students. Some turned back to look at her. Adriana heard the comments: «She's his wife. . . She came yesterday. . .» They also nodded to her, smiling. Next to her a drunk took out a knife and cried,

«All right, you bastard, let's see who has the balls.»

She shrank against Tino's shoulder and he murmured,

«Don't be afraid. . . Nothing's going to happen.»

When they arrived at the entrance to the Emir, Tino turned to look at her and embraced her.

«You're scared to death! Silly!»

«Won't they hurt each other?» she asked.

«No. If anyone were hurt, there would be a terrible hassle. Come on. . . We'll go find them.»

«Please introduce us to your wife!»

Tino turned around. He nodded to the group and they applauded.

She felt obliged to laugh; they were watching her. She also nodded to them.

«Who are they?» she asked following him again.

«They're from the Symphony and the Theater School . . . Look, there's Leandro!»

«My God!» she cried, «he's going to fall!»

But three masqueraders caught him first.

When they finally got to the table, Leandro was serving drinks to the masqueraders.

«Better give my wife some linden tea,» Tino said. «She's been scared out of her wits seven times between the house and here.»

«It's just that,» she explained laughing, «. . . all this is a little overwhelming for me. . . Well, anyway, a little unusual.»

«When you've lived here a whole year,» Barbara said, «it will all seem very natural.»

«Yes,» Bartolomé explained. «it's. . . a kind of exorcism for the Jalapans.»

«And for the ones who are not Jalapans,» Barbara declared. «All of us need this and at times I think we outsiders need it most.»

«Don't exaggerate!» Tino protested. «Jalapa is not as boring as that.»

«Well,» Adriana said, accepting the drink Leandro gave her, «I would say that as far as I can see, it's not a *bit* boring.»

«Yes, but all this gaity,» Bartolomé said, «*fortunately* doesn't last all year.»

«*Fortunately,* Sara emphasized.

She was shouting in order to be heard over the noise of the orchestra that was playing:

Rock, rock, rock the baby, now. . .

and the mariachis:

> One dark and quiet night
> You swore to love forever
> You said through all your life
> You'd leave me never ever.

and the marimba:

> On this clear night of sparkling stars
> I've come to say how much I love you.

* * *

As she was passing by the tavern the redheaded witch was lifted bodily by a drunk.

«Up you go, little witch!» he cried picking her up. He put her down suddenly and before letting her go, put his hand on her breast. He whispered.

«You're not a boy, are you?»

She wasn't. The drunk smiled, paying no attention to the witch's howls. «Come have a drink with me!»

«I can't!» she cried in a falsetto voice. «I can't because of my mask!»

«You'll have a drink with me or I'll tear your mask off!»

«I'll have one, my lord, I'll have one! But don't order me around!»

«Chucho! Two beers!»

The witch gave the drunk a kiss while they waited for the beers. She laughed a little because he tickled her and tried to rub up against her. Finally she let him hug her.

«Ah, little witch. . . my little witch.»

She kissed him again. He snuggled against her.

«Four pesos!» Chucho said.

Still laughing the witch put the bottle to the mouth of her rubber mask. Some of the beer slid down her face but she paid no attention.

They both finished it without stopping. The drunk was young — «a railroad man» she thought.

«Shall I take off your mask?» he asked tenderly, while he held her close.

«No!» she screamed. «My husband is around here! . . . No!»

He kissed her.

«But wait for me here. I'll come back. . . I swear I'll come back . . . Do you have a place somewhere?» and she kissed him.

«You come back and you'll see.»

The witch ran into the street splashing mud, shrieking and laughing wildly. Can it be true? Will he wait for me? She hesitated for a few moments, thought of returning immediately and then kept on running, jumping and throwing confetti. She went down the main street. Her courage increased. She kept dancing and entered the Casino. A group of young people were leaving a table. The witch ran toward them crying.

«You don't know me! You don't know me!»

Daniel recognized her. She was the witch who had rescued him from the flannel cats.

«I saved him for you, Alicia Esteva!» the witch screamed. «I saved him for you! If it hadn't been for me, they would have stolen him! Right, handsome?»

The group started walking away. The witch ran behind them and caught the hand of Jacobo who was alone.

«No, no! Dummies! I'm going with you!»

«Alicia, Carmela! We're coming, too!» the can-can dancers cried and both joined the group.

Alma watched their friends go out and put her head on Arnaldo's shoulder.

* * *

Dancing the conga they moved boisterously along Calle Real with

Carmela at the head, Hernán second and the can-can dancers bringing up the rear.

Six lessons from Madam Lazonga

* * *

Oblivious to the drizzle and fog, making their way through the crowd and gathering confetti insults laughter streamers, they went into Enriquez Arcade and burst into El Escorial. The owner and waiters didn't know what to do. Entrance was forbidden to masqueraders but these came with familiar people — the daughter of Don Luis Esteva . . . — they let them in, and the masqueraders, determined to make a scene, whooped it up until everybody paid attention to them. A brief silence was broken by a horrible shriek. The silence grew heavy again. Then a repetition of the shriek in a wordless confusion

«E-e-e-e-e-e-e!»

«E-e-e-e-e-e-e!»

«Let's go, Christi!»

«Come on Loli, come on!»

«Society rejects us!»

Together, plaintively, «They are criticizing us!»

And the ballerinas took the stage and started to dance. Laughter solved everything. Color came back to the owner's face. He was afraid, for a while, that someone had been killed. The waiters held their stomachs and laughed happily. The ballerinas knew lots of steps and did them all perfectly. The witch and Jacobo, applauding, kept time with the dance. Streamers fell all over them. For a moment El Escorial became a happy place.

* * *

«Me? . . I'll be the bodyguard!» Carlín said cheerfully.

The three of them, wearing hoods, started walking toward Calle Enriquez.

* * *

«Impossible,» Barbara said, sitting down again.

Bartolomé sat down too, and immediately picked up his glass.

«No!» he said. «It can't be done!»

«You can't tell whether you're dancing or just keeping your balance between pushes.»

«You'd better not try,» Sara said to Leandro, patting his cheek lovingly.

«You either,» Adriana said to Tino.

«She's saying that because she thinks it's a sin to dance during Lent.»

«Tino!» she interrupted.

He disregarded her and kept on.

«Seeing somebody dance is kind of a sin. Right, beautiful?» He planted a kiss on her cheek and kept on for the benefit of the others. «They brought her up for me in a convent school.»

«'Bourgeois pettiness and restraint', as our good friend Wells would say,» (Leandro)

«Don't mention the schools in Puebla.»

«O.K. I know the ones in Monterrey are worse.»

«You always quote Arnaldo,» Sara shouted, «whenever you don't dare say something yourself.»

«We'll put that comment aside for a better occasion,» Leandro said.

«Bravo for our local poet!» Bartolomé said. Then confidentially but still shouting, to Sara, «Did you know he used to write poetry years ago?» . . . Ballads. . . Let's see. . . Leandro! . . Recite something for us. . .»

Leandro stood up immediately and began,

> The heavens melt in somber weeping
> for three sad girls, in silence keeping
> grief calm, but not concealing
> their tonic souls and fragrant feeling.
> The heavens melt in somber weeping.

A bottle passed within a hair's breadth of Leandro's head and shattered against the wall. Two prep school students were fighting. The police, covered with confetti, came up to separate them.

Bartolomé continued,

«You see? . . His poetry is so controversial there are those who try to kill him. They are, it might be said in passing, admirers of García Lorca, because although your husband swears if there are similarities between himself and García Lorca, it is only coincidental, few are prepared to accept it. Come on, Leandro, do 'I took her away by the river. . .' No, excuse me, that's not one of yours! But it's so much like yours!»

«Ah!» Leandro exclaimed, laughing. «You're no fool but you're always fooling around!»

«That guy!» Bartolomé said to Adriana. «He always has to plagiarize someone. The brilliant sentence he just uttered is one of mine.»

* * *

After the show the group went out into the street again, still in a twisting line. Now the can-can dancers were in the lead. They left Enriquez Arcade and in a perfect diagonal proceeded toward Tanos Arcade. In spite of the crush they were able to move without difficulty. The people let them through, saying, «Look, look!»

And the can-can dancers lifted their skirts and showed their red-black mesh stockings, singing stridently,

> From Plateros to Colon
> they go riding, riding on
> riding on
> on their bicycle
> built for two.

«With these shock troopers,» Luis said to Margarita, «everyone gives us an open road.»

They reached the entrance of the Emir and the dancers won still another victory: the crowd opened to make a small gap which they penetrated shrieking. The invasion ended at Leandro and Bartolomé's table. The dancers ran to kiss Leandro.

«You don't know me!»

«You don't know me!»

The witch also kissed him and said,

«You don't know me!»

* * *

«We'll be married on Easter Sunday,» Arnaldo said.

Alma burst out laughing. She felt like a small animal freed for the first time: happy for the first time as if a jail or trap had just opened. She didn't believe a word and couldn't do anything but laugh and look at him. Her whole being was almost crystal and a long moment passed before she moved close to Arnaldo's lips and gave him a brief kiss.

«Arnaldo. . . Arnaldo. . . Professor Wells. . . Yes, I will marry you. Yes!»

They looked at each other for a long time.

Then, without saying a word, they stood up and, arms interlocked, went walking down the street.

* * *

Felipe Gómez grabbed his friend and pulled him into the main street. «Come on,» he said, «we haven't found anything. . .»

Isidro Nervo decided to follow him. He bought a kilo sack of confetti and started throwing it on all the women: he didn't care about age height beauty ugliness acceptance rejection. Later he bought some leis and put them on very proudly.

«You look like a woman,» Felip Gómez told him.

«A woman is what I want,» he answered, taking a handful of confetti.

«You can't find one you're a . . .»

Before he could finish, the handful of confetti was in his mouth. Isidro shook with laughter.

«I found you! You're my . . .! Look out. Don't choke! It can't be that bad!»

Felipe Gómez, with confetti down his throat, was vomiting. When the seizure passed, he pushed Isidro Nervo who was slapping him on the back.

«Stop it! Get away from me! I've had about enough of you!»

At first Isidro was surprised, thinking he was joking, but then he saw his annoyed expression.

«But I. . .»

Felipe Gómez started walking toward Tanos Arcade without turning to see if the other were following him. Isidro ran to catch up with him. What's going on? he asked himself. We always go around together. He caught up and explained,

«It was just a handful of confetti.»

«Go to hell.»

«But. . .» Isidro ran to catch up again. They had gone everywhere together for ten years. He grabbed his arm and asked,

«Aren't we buddies any more?»

«Draw your gun!» Felipe Gómez ordered.

Isidro smiled, slapped him on the shoulder and pulled a bottle of rum from his back pocket. They both took a drink.

* * *

The witch said to Jacobo,

«Come on, let's dance.»

«I'll come back on a broom in a little while,» Jacobo said, following her.

* * *

«There they are. . .» Alma said pointing to the group.

«Come on,» Arnaldo said.

* * *

Luis and Margarita went over to Bartolomé. Luis said, «We're going to get married this week-end.»

«Boo!» Batuta yelled in Alicia's face. «I've looked all over Jalapa for you!»

«Well, sit down. . .» she said. «As if we had a choice!»

The noise was so deafening sometimes it seemed that nobody would be able to stand it. The waitresses could no longer serve their customers. They mixed up the orders, forgot to collect from people who hadn't paid, and made others pay double. Policemen were everywhere but they paid less and less attention to maintaining order. There were friends everywhere! Everybody was a friend at that moment and anybody could become an enemy immediately. Confetti streamers bottles and glasses falling to the floor. People in masks running from table to table yelling insults laughing dancing making somebody fall down. It is impossible to tell what they are singing or what they are dancing.

Suddenly there was single noise — a great round of applause. The people who were sitting down didn't know what. . . who. Everybody stood up as the applause grew louder. Some stood on their chairs so they could see.

«It's Fidel!»

«Viva Cuba!»

«Down with the gringos!»

«Viva Cuba!»

«Viva!»

A group of masqueraders — Fidel and his militia (male and female) were making their triumphal entry.

A single cheer, intense, authentic, in unison,

«Viva Cuba, viva Cuba, viva Cuba!»

* * *

A masquerader came running up and stopped at the statue of Sebastián Lerdo de Tejada. He turned to look behind — no one was following. Discreetly, he coughed as if suffocated. Then with difficulty he put his hands in his pocket to get out cigarettes. He kept on coughing as he lighted one. The noise was deafening and the drizzle continued. He sneezed.

A woman wearing a mask ran into the small park and also stopped next to the statue. She also looked behind. No one — that is, the park was full of people but no one, no one in a hood, was following her. She went up to him.

«Is it you?» she asked.

«No. . . It's me.»

Zenaida recognized his hand.

«What shall we do?»

«This is ridiculous!» he protested. «Let's go to bed!»

«But maybe he's waiting for us in the car,» she said.

«Then we can get a taxi,» Genaro said. «We're disguised.»

* * *

The ballerinas were making everyone laugh. One of them had three drinks one after the other. Now both of them in a mechanical rhythm, as if they had practiced for years, were moving their heads to the right left down up up down, while they sang. Their wigs were stuck to the stockings they wore over their faces.

I'm telling you no, I'm saying no
cause I have me a beau
so I'm telling you no, I'm saying no
his name is Antonio.

«Who are they?» Daniel asked Alicia in a low voice.

«I don't know,» she answered also in a low voice. «But I'm sure they're people I know.»

* * *

«Hi, buddy! Don't you remember me?»

Felipe Gómez stopped next to Hernán, who didn't recognize him. He stood looking at him trying to remember.

«Yes!» Luis shouted, explaining to Hernán, «Our friends. . . yesterday in Antonio's cantina.»

«Of course!» Hernán exclaimed. He stood up and shook hands with both, then introduced them, «Gentlemen . . . some friends. . .»

«Felipe Gómez, your servant, and my friend, Isidro Nervo.»

Everyone shook hands.

Leandro passed the bottle so they could serve themselves.

They touched glasses. Felipe Gómez asked about Jacobo, «And the other one, where is he?»

«Dancing,» Hernán said. «Cheers!»

Isidro Nervo looked at the huge room jammed with people — suddenly, very close and walking in a straight line toward him, he saw the red-headed witch again.

The witch cried out in surprise. It was too late to go back; «the same man here,» she said to herself in confusion. Isidro Nervo smiled. Jacobo took the witch's hand and gave her a drink. She covered her fright with little leaps here and there finally stopping near Isidro Nervo.

«There may be trouble ahead!» she started singing. «There may be trou-

ble ahead. I'll drink no more! I'm going to my little nest! Right away!»
Isidro Nervo moved close to Felipe Gómez and they talked secretly.
«I'm going! I'm going to my nest. It's late!»
No one stopped her and she went out slowly.
Before she reached the main street, Isidro Nervo caught up with her and took her arm.
«Let's dance first,» she begged in a shrill voice. «One piece and then I'll go with you.»
Isidro grabbed her, held her body tightly to his and tried to follow the rhythm of the music.

* * *

Cristi tapped Loli and in a low voice said,
«I can't stand this stocking any more. I'm melting. Let's go.»
«O.K. Let's go before they recognize us.»
Cristi was the first to get up. Her piercing voice dominated the uproar,
«And now, my dears, at the request of numerous friends, Loli and I will dance.»
They put their arms around each other's shoulders. With their free hands they picked up their skirts and making little leaps, they began:

> I am the captain of
> the bravest company-y-y-y
> I am the captain of
> the bravest company-y-y-y
> Oh, oh, my dear captain. . .
> Oh, oh, my dear captain.

They advanced miraculously without a hitch and disappeared swallowed up in the crowd.
«But,» Sara cried, «who are they?»
No one knew. Leandro said,
«I don't know who *they* are, but I am sure the witch was my Aunt Clementina.»
«No!»
«Clemen!»
Everyone shouted with laughter.
«But she. . .»
«So lively!»
«Why didn't she ever get married?»
«Because she didn't want to. That's the only reason.»

«Well,» Sara put in, «I think there's something more, it's not as easy as that. You have to realize her Jalapa is the Jalapa of twenty years ago. . . Anyway, I'm sure there are extenuating circumstances.»

* * *

The waiter placed a bottle of brandy and one of whisky on the table.
«Who ordered these?» Bartolomé asked.
«A gift from Batuta,» Alicia said.
Batuta smiled.
«We've had it,» Jacobo exclaimed shurgging his shoulders. «We can't drink another drop.»
«They've drunk like pigs!» Carmela said.
«You girls, too.»
«It's Carnival!» Batuta cried pouring for everyone. «It happens only once a year.»
«If you keep on like this,» Hernán told him, «not just once a year, but more often, if every month you give us whisky and cognac, we'll let you be our friend. Even if you are an ass. . .»
«Cheers for. . . what's your name?» Tino asked.
«Carlos Zamora,» Batuta said.
«Point of order!» Arnaldo Wells cried. «Be quiet, please! . . Alma and I are going to be married on Easter Sunday. . .»
«A toast to the newlyweds!»
Everyone applauded.
«Another motion!» Luis called.
«Better said — emotion.» Jacobo interrupted.
«All right, emotion! Margarita and I are also going to be married — next Saturday.»
«Cheers for the bride and groom!»
I'll give them a blender, Batuta thought.
«I like this,» Adriana said waving to the large group around the table. «In Mexico City you couldn't. . . there isn't. . . This communication, this comaraderie.»
Barbara commented sarcastically, «But at times the camaraderie overflows and our husbands don't behave as well as their students.»
«It doesn't matter!» Hernán interrupted. «It doesn't matter that the professors are not respectable as long as we respect them.»
«You're going to get zero!» Jacobo yelled.
«And that's about right.» (Daniel)
«Man, even Daniel spoke up!»

«It's not his fault,» Jacobo put in. «Alicia won't let his mouth alone.»
«Idiot!»
«I'm not lying. . . Look at him. . . at least wipe off his face.»
Alicia wiped Daniel's mouth.
In the men's room another fight started.

* * *

The ballerinas were running. When they reached the corner, they stopped and, joining hands, darted along another street going downhill. They rounded the next corner toward the left and then after another block, turned right. They passed in front of the great oak entrance of Dr. Pereda's house and continued running to the corner. There suddenly they stopped. The silence was absolute. No one else was anywhere in the street. They went back to the oak entrance and both went in quickly, laughing. Again they ran while taking off stocking masks and wigs. Their faces were moist and red. In the living room they fell on the couch and kicked off their shoes.
«I've never had such a good time!» Clementina exclaimed.
«We were stupendous!» Borrito agreed.
«And no one recognized us!»

* * *

Exhausted from so much running, Carlín sat on a bench.
«They are going to pay for this!» he swore clenching his teeth. «They are going to pay for this!»

* * *

The Cathedral clock struck three in the morning. The music had stopped and the rain as well. A cold wind swept through the almost empty streets. Cars were passing by, full of people singing laughing or quarreling.
«We'll do it again tomorrow!» someone cried. «We still have two more days! Come on!»

* * *

The witch kept on laughing and without letting him take off her mask retreated into a corner of the hotel room.
«I'll take if off after you undress,» she said.
Isidro Nervo undressed quickly in front of her. The witch trembled and removed her mask.

He didn't recognize her, never had seen her before, and even if Alicia Esteva herself had entered the room at that moment, she could not have recognized Señora Isunza — the harassed and always frightened Señora Isunza who was her housekeeper.

She also undressed rapidly.

The door to the hall opened. Terrified she turned and looked at Isidro, who was smiling. Felipe Gómez started to undress.

«It's Carnival,» she told herself. «It's Carnival.»

* * *

«I miss the children,» Adriana said leaning against his shoulder.

«I'm the one you should be missing,» Tino responded.

Adriana laughed quietly. He saw her laugh as they came to a lighted crossing.

«At this moment I need *you* more than anyone,» she said and kissed his hand.

«Hurrah for Jalapa, my wife has just declared she loves me!»

«Lucky man!» Leandro said. «My wife has just declared war on me!»

«And my wife,» Bartolomé said, «has just declared silence, thank God.»

In the back seat — Tino, Adriana, Bartolomé and Barbara. Leandro was driving. At his side Sara leaned over and kissed his cheek.

«The war is over,» she whispered.

«The one who is going to have trouble is Genaro,» Bartolomé said. And later added, «I'd like to be him.»

«*Cheri. . . cheri. . .*» Barbara exclaimed, «wait your turn. . . I've never been selfish but confusion bothers me. And three make confusion.»

«Don't pay attention to them,» Tino told Adriana. «They're pretending to be 'jet set'.»

«Now when we get to the bridge, we will die.»

«And tomorrow my aunt will send a wreath.»

«Are you sure the place is open at this hour?»

«Of course. The police haven't closed it yet.»

The car shot forward. A beautiful moon burst forth. The curtain of clouds pulled back suddenly and clear moonlight flooded the road.

Behind them the city hidden within its different levels started quieting down. The moon rose calmly over its sleep.